south side sports

high *and inside*

Jeff Rud

ORCA BOOK PUBLISHERS

Library and Archives Canada Cataloguing in Publication

Rud, Jeff, 1960-
High and inside / Jeff Rud.

(South Side sports; #2)
ISBN 1-55143-532-2
I. Title. II. Series.

PS8635.U32H53 2006   jC813'.6   C2006-901307-1

Summary: Twelve-year-old Matt must learn to face a high and inside pitch
while dealing with allegiances to friends and doing the right thing.

First published in the United States, 2006
Library of Congress Control Number: 2006922295

Orca Book Publishers gratefully acknowledges the support for its publishing
programs provided by the following agencies: the government of Canada
through the Book Publishing Industry Development Program (BPIDP), the
Canada Council for the Arts, the government of British Columbia and the
British Columbia Arts Council.

Cover design: John van der Woude
Cover photography: Getty Images

Orca Book Publishers
PO Box 5626, Stn B.
Victoria, BC Canada
V8R 6S4

Orca Book Publishers
PO Box 468
Custer, WA USA
98240-0468

Printed and bound in Canada
www.orcabook.com

08 07 06 • 5 4 3 2 1

For Auntie Betty,
who will be dearly missed by many.

Acknowledgments

Thanks to editor Andrew Wooldridge and publisher Bob Tyrrell for their guidance and support; and to all the players at Fireman's Park for providing inspiration.

chapter one

The baseball left the pitcher's hand in a white blur, hurtling toward Matthew Hill. Instinctively Matt ducked his slender shoulders and lurched backward, stumbling slightly as he retreated from the batter's box.

Matt heard the snickers coming from the dugout behind him. And he could anticipate what was coming next. "Don't back away, son," Coach Jim Stephens said firmly from down the first-base line. "You can't hit it if you don't even swing the bat."

"C'mon, Hill," laughed the lanky teammate who had tossed the pitch. It had been a slightly high fastball that had ultimately split the heart of the plate. "I'm only throwing three-quarter speed. Don't be afraid of the ball."

Afraid of the ball! There, somebody had actually said it out loud. Matt Hill was afraid of the baseball. This was humiliating. If only he had a shovel in his hand instead of a bat; then at least he could pry up home plate and crawl underneath it.

It was just a practice, the final one for the South Side Stingers varsity baseball team before the regular season began. But it felt like Game Seven of the World Series as far as Matt was concerned. And the seventh-grade rookie had just struck out looking. Worse than that, he had struck out ducking. And now to top things off, everybody on the team knew he was afraid of the ball.

The black-haired boy on the mound was Steve White, a ninth-grader with a bit of an attitude and the South Side team's pitching ace. It was just batting practice, but Matt was nevertheless nervous standing in the box against the lefty, who was one of the fastest pitchers in the city. White's stuff was certainly much faster than any of the chuckers Matt had faced in Little League.

He dug in again, sinking his cleats into the soft clay of the batter's box and getting set for the next pitch. He was determined to hang in there this time and not back away, no matter what happened. White went into his long, deliberate windup. It seemed like forever, but in fact it was only a couple of seconds before the older boy uncoiled and sent the ball again in a flash toward the plate.

This time Matt stayed in the box, swinging at the spot where he anticipated the baseball would cross. But this pitch was slightly inside. It nicked him on the index finger of his right hand and ricocheted off his cheekbone. The pain shot through his finger and the left side of his face at the same time, but Matt stayed on his feet.

"Uhhhh," he groaned. Somehow he stifled the urge to cry, but he couldn't hold it in completely.

"You okay, Matt?" said Coach Stephens, a look of concern crossing his angular face. He hurried toward the plate. The coach examined Matt's swelling cheek for a few seconds and then patted him on the back. "You'd better go take a seat for awhile in the dugout. Have Charlie get you some ice."

"Sorry, Hill," yelled White from the mound. He didn't sound overly sorry. "It was an accident, man."

Matt nodded. He turned and walked toward the dugout, handing his bat to Charles Dougan, the South Side team manager. Dougan was a small blond boy with a brace on his left leg that filled up the entire space between where his blue gym shorts ended and his white sock began. He grabbed the bat from Matt and added it to the collection he had arranged in meticulous order—from smallest to largest—by sticking their handles into the chain-link fence.

Matt took a seat in the dugout. Charlie plopped down beside him, momentarily forgetting the coach's call for ice and instead staring intently out at the plate. Everybody on the South Side team was watching the same thing. Up next for his cuts at batting practice was Jake Piancato, one of Matt's best friends and the purest hitting member of the Stingers. It was only practice, but everybody was eager to watch Piancato try to get the best of White in this matchup.

Steve White stared at Jake from the mound, his dark eyes seeming more intense than they had minutes earlier when Matt had been at the plate. White again went into his windup and practically threw his entire body forward as he delivered the ball toward Jake. It was obvious that White didn't want Piancato to hit the ball, practice or not.

Jake didn't flinch. He stood in there strong, taking a hard but controlled swing and sending the baseball on a crackling rope into right field for what probably would have been a stand-up double in any real game.

"Nice poke, Piancato," Coach Stephens shouted. "Give him a couple more, White, and remember, the object here is just to throw strikes, not to get strikeouts. Save that stuff for the games."

Crimson rose on White's cheeks. He was easily South Side's best pitcher this season. But he wasn't the team's best player. That honor, beyond a doubt, went to Jake. This at-bat was simply reinforcing that fact. Even White had to admit it, but he didn't have to like it.

For as long as Matt had known Jake—which was practically as far back as he could remember—his blond curly-haired friend had been a natural athlete, good at whatever he tried. So good, in fact, that sometimes it seemed as though Jake didn't have to try very hard at all.

In no sport, though, was he more naturally talented than baseball. This was Jake's game. Not only had he been one of the city's best hitters as a Little Leaguer, he was also a terrific shortstop, able to cover much of the infield with his natural, bouncy athleticism. Despite the fact that, like Matt, he was just a first-year seventh-grader at South Side, Jake had dominated early-season practice sessions for the Stingers in almost every way.

Steve White bore down on the mound again, narrowed his eyes on the target and fired another pitch toward the plate. He had taken nothing off this one, despite the coach's advice. But to Jake it was as if the lefty's fastball was moving in slow motion. His bat ripped forward, his weight transferring perfectly from his legs through his impressive forearms. This time the ball arced high over the white wooden right-field fence, disappearing into some lilac bushes that lined the school diamond.

"Ka-jaccka," yelled South Side catcher, Phil Wong, imitating the local late-night sportscaster who punctuated every major league home run highlight with that annoying, incomprehensible word. "What have you been eating for breakfast, Jaker?"

A smile crossed Jake's lips and his blue eyes danced, lighting up the broad face framed by curls. But this wasn't a cocky grin. It was merely a reflection of the joy of being able to do something well. It wasn't in Jake's nature to want to show somebody up.

Matt had to smile too, at the sight of his friend being so dominant at the plate. But at the same time, his own performance gnawed at him. He had played well enough in the field during pre-season practices for the South Side squad, but he had been consistently nervous at the plate and today was no exception. It was true what his teammates were quietly saying about him; he was afraid of the baseball—at least he was whenever a fast pitcher was delivering it. And getting hit in the hand and on the cheek today wasn't going to make the next trip to the plate against White, or any other fireballer, any easier.

"That's enough, guys," Coach Stephens said, obviously feeling that Jake's over-the-fence shot had provided a proper punctuation to practice. "Let's bring it in. Good workout today. I just want a few words and then you can all take off home."

The sun was beginning to dip in the spring sky and the air had that sweet, fresh-cut-grass smell that made everything seem alive and full of promise. Baseball season was just starting and summer vacation wouldn't be far behind. Matt loved this time of year.

"Okay, boys, listen up," Coach Stephens said. "We've got North Vale on Monday in our opener. They're going to be tough this year, but so are we. Have a good weekend, relax and spend some time with your friends and families. But I want you all here Monday at 4:00 PM, prepared to play some heads-up baseball. Is everybody ready?"

Maroon ball caps nodded all around.

"I said, is everybody ready?"

"Yes sir!" This time the South Side players shouted back in unison.

"I can't hear you," Coach said playfully.

"YES SIR!" they screamed.

"That's more like it."

The South Side players headed for the locker room, excited about their first game being just a few days away. Matt walked across the field with Jake and Phil, two of his best friends since pre-school days. The three had played baseball all through Little League and now they had moved up together to middle school ball.

"What's up, Matty?" Phil asked, noticing how quiet he had been.

"Only that I stink," Matt replied. "I don't know what it is. All of a sudden, I just can't hit."

"Don't worry," Jake said reassuringly. "You're just getting used to the speed of middle school pitching. You'll be okay once you adjust."

"For sure," Phil added. "It is a lot faster."

Matt nodded. It was nice of his friends to try to make him feel better. But inside, he wasn't so sure they were right this time. Neither of them was having much trouble hitting the baseball so far during South Side practices. So why was he?

The three boys showered and changed and headed home down Anderson Crescent together just as they had always done since their early school days at nearby Glenview. When they reached Matt's block, he said goodbye to his buddies and was heading toward his house when he heard a familiar voice calling from behind.

"Hey, Matt. Hold up a second."

It was Neil Peters, a neighbor, out for a walk with his dog, Joker. Neil was a city police officer with the canine squad and Joker, a sleek black German Shepherd, lived with the Peters family when the two weren't on duty. Matt often ran into Officer Peters and his dog on their street. It seemed to him that Joker got a walk at least four times a day.

Matt bent over to pat Joker's soft, noble head. The shepherd's ears stood straight up, almost as if they were at attention. Joker was a beautiful dog, smart and extremely well-trained. But he wasn't a pet in the normal sense of the word. He was a working dog, and Officer Peters and Joker were partners.

"You just coming from practice?" the policeman asked. "How's the team looking anyway?"

Officer Peters loved baseball and had even coached Matt, Jake and Phil for a couple of seasons early on in Little League. He had been the one who had first shown Matt how to throw a baseball properly, how to step, turn and deliver so that he got maximum power sending the ball across the infield to first base.

"I think we'll be pretty good," Matt replied. "Jake's pounding it already, and I think Phil's going to start at catcher. And we've got some decent pitching..."

"How about you? Where's the coach playing you?"

"Second, mostly," Matt said. "And some outfield." He didn't want to mention the problems he was having at the plate. Enough people on the South Side team already knew he was afraid of the ball.

"Well, have a good weekend," Officer Peters said. "I'm taking Joker for his workout. Say hi to your mom for me."

Matt watched as the policeman and Joker moved away. The sleek black dog stayed tight by Officer Peters' side, even though he wasn't on a leash, and the two "partners" moved as one. Every few steps, the husky brown-haired officer would stop and so would Joker. The shepherd would then look up at his master and wait for the command before proceeding or even so much as moving a paw.

Officer Peters and his family had lived on their block since before Matt, his mother and his older brother Mark had moved in a few years back. Having a police officer just a couple of doors down had always made his family feel a little more secure. But strangely it had also made Matt feel slightly nervous at times too. Although he'd never broken the law, Matt was keenly aware that he'd better not even think about it with Officer Peters and Joker around.

chapter two

Matt woke up excited the next morning. It was springtime; it was Saturday; and baseball season was set to start in two days.

But it was more than that. This weekend he had been invited out to the Piancatos' resort on nearby Long Lake. Jake's parents had made a yearly habit of taking some of their son's friends to their lodge for a May weekend, just before the resort started getting busy for another tourist season. Typically, Jake and his buddies had the run of the docks, swimming area, the canoes and the property. It was always a lot of fun and had become a spring tradition to which Matt looked forward.

He had packed his bag the night before, wanting to make sure he was ready to go when the Piancatos arrived. Matt had his swimsuit, although he knew the lake would be cold. He had extra jeans and T-shirts and socks and his down-filled sleeping bag.

He and Jake would be sharing one of the guest cabins for the weekend. It was going to be a blast.

Sitting at the kitchen table in his family's modest two-bedroom house, Matt heard a car horn just as he finished his second piece of toast. His mom heard it too. "That's Jake's parents," she said. "Are you all ready to go?"

Matt nodded. He picked up his gear and headed for the door. His petite auburn-haired mother wasn't far behind him. "You'd better give me a kiss here," she smiled warmly, rising on her toes to kiss her son on the forehead. "I don't want to embarrass you in front of your friend."

Matt gave his mom a big hug, a peck on the cheek and an extra little squeeze. "Make sure you remember your manners and behave yourself up there," she said. "Remember, it's a privilege to get the chance to go."

"I know, Mom," Matt said, a trace of weariness in his voice. "Don't worry, I will. You don't have to tell me that every time I go somewhere, you know."

They were at the front door, and Jake's parents had pulled the familiar long red station wagon with the brown wood paneling into their driveway. Mom waved and smiled at the Piancatos. Because he and Jake had been friends forever, their parents knew each other pretty well too. Jake's mom and dad smiled back from the front seat.

Jake was in the backseat, but he swung open the station-wagon door, jumped out and hollered. "Hey Mattster! Are you ready for the Long Lake Monster? Because he's ready for you!" Jake was holding a stuffed, plush, green sea serpent and waving it toward him menacingly. Inside the car, Jake's parents shared a quiet giggle. The Long Lake Monster had been a standing joke between the Piancatos and Matt ever since the first time he had visited their lodge and been too scared to go into the water because he thought it was inhabited by sea monsters. But at the time, Matt was just five years old and had never swum in a lake before. He was twelve going on thirteen now and had grown to love the cool clear water of Long Lake.

The resort was just five miles outside of town, so it would only take a few minutes to get there. But every time Matt visited, he felt like he was hours removed from the city. Long Lake had been designated by the government as a protected area and development had been limited to just the Long Lake Lodge, the Piancatos' small resort, and a number of family cabins strung around the serene lake. The cabins were spaced out, and the lake was framed by towering stands of pine that created a feeling of wilderness even though it was so near the heart of the city. There was a large public beach with a picnic area and campground next to the lodge, so anybody could enjoy Long Lake, but motorboats weren't permitted on the water, meaning that it was usually fairly quiet. It had become one of Matt's very favorite places in the world. Jake was awfully lucky to live out there all year-round, he thought for probably the five-hundredth time.

Matt sat in the backseat with Jake, surrounded by bedding, supplies and stacks of non-perishable food, items the Piancatos were taking out to the lodge this weekend as they worked to prepare for the upcoming busy guest season. Mr. Piancato was a large, balding man in his fifties who had the same easy-going smile as his son and a crazy sense of humor. Mrs. Piancato was a gentle, pretty woman who had been like a second mother to Matt over the years. Looking at her, it was obvious where Jake got his curly blond hair and blue eyes.

Matt really felt comfortable with the Piancatos. He surveyed the three of them and couldn't help thinking—also for about the five-hundredth time—that Jake was fortunate to have both a mom and a dad in his life.

Not that Matt felt particularly shortchanged. His mother was about as supportive and understanding as any parent could be. It's just that sometimes he wondered how it would feel to have a dad at home too. His own father had left the family when Matt was just three, too early for him to remember much. They had had no contact since, and he and his mother seldom talked about it.

Matt's thoughts were interrupted by Jake. "We're going to have some company at the lake this weekend," he said enthusiastically. "My cousins are going to be there too. Since Phil and Amar couldn't make it, Mom invited Cody and Vance up for the weekend."

Matt's heart sunk. He already knew that Phil and Amar Sunir—the others in he and Jake's crowd—weren't able to come along this weekend because of other commitments. But he had assumed that he and Jake would be able to hang out on their own at Long Lake. Now he was learning that Cody and Vance were coming too. Matt had met Jake's cousins before, and he had never hit it off with them.

"Er, great," Matt said, mustering as much fake enthusiasm as he could. "How old are those guys now?"

"Cody is fourteen and Vance is nearly sixteen," Mrs. Piancato interjected pleasantly from the front seat. "We haven't seen them for awhile. But their parents are in Mexico for a couple of weeks, and so we offered to take care of the boys while they're gone. Jake's dad drove up to Eton and picked them up early this morning. They're already out at the lake. Jake hasn't even seen his cousins yet because he stayed in town last night with his aunt."

Although he was disappointed, Matt felt like he managed to hide it. Besides, maybe he would get along better with Jake's cousins now that everybody was a little older. He could give it a shot at least.

"I see the lake," yelled Jake, winning the game that the Piancatos always played in the car. The first person to see any tinge of blue through the trees on the winding road into Long Lake was the winner. And the winner got to skip unloading the gear once they arrived.

Mr. Piancato pulled the station wagon past the public beach and into the driveway of the Long Lake Lodge. The resort was modest, consisting of one main building and a dozen quaint satellite cabins, all constructed from massive logs. But each of the units was well-appointed inside with a fireplace, down-filled comforters and pillows and a full four-piece bathroom. And each of them had a comfortable veranda to sit on and watch the sun set over Long Lake.

The car stopped, and Matt hopped out, stretching his legs and arms. He always loved the smell at the Piancatos' lodge, the crisp, slightly cooler air and the shade of the big pines. It was the same every time he came. So relaxing.

"Duuude!" The peace was shattered by a voice coming from the main lodge. Jake's cousin Cody was headed toward them. "Man, Cuz, you've grown up a bit."

Jake blushed, looking back at Cody, who stood about two inches taller and had straight blond hair hanging nearly to his shoulders. Cody was wearing a black *Green Day* T-shirt and long, skater-style, purple shorts. Matt couldn't help noticing he had a gold ring in his left earlobe.

Matt felt awkward. Picking up on the situation, Mrs. Piancato cleared her throat. "Jake, did you introduce Matt to Cody?"

"This is Matt?" Cody exclaimed. "Little Matt? This is the same kid who we met out here a couple of years ago? The kid who was scared of the lake monster?"

Jake nodded. It was Matt's turn to blush now. How long was that Long Lake Monster thing going to stick with him, anyway?

"You're a lot bigger too," Cody said.

Matt felt a little more at ease—for a second, that is.

Around the corner of the main lodge came Vance, Jake's older cousin. He wasn't smiling. About the same height as Cody, Vance had long, shiny, black hair and was dressed in black jeans, red sneakers and a black sweatshirt with a skull and crossbones logo. He looked at the Piancatos and Matt but said nothing.

"Hey, Vance," said Mr. Piancato. "Are you finding your way around here okay?"

"I guess," shrugged the teenager. "Just looking for something to do."

"Perfect," Mr. Piancato replied. "I've got a whole car here to unload. So let's get to it boys."

Mr. Piancato and the boys, except for Jake who had won the I-see-the-lake contest, unloaded the station wagon, while Mrs. Piancato went directly into the lodge. When the chores were finished, Jake asked Matt if he wanted to check out the lake. "Sure," Matt replied. "Let's go see if that monster's still down there."

The two laughed. Across the driveway, Vance was giving them a slightly quizzical look. "What's the joke, man?" he said to Jake.

Jake started to remind Vance about Matt's previous fears of the Long Lake Monster and how it was still a standing joke in the family but he didn't get quite finished before Vance interrupted. "Whatever, man," he said. "What do you guys do for fun around here?"

Matt and Jake looked at each other. What did he mean fun? It was a lake, wasn't it? Did they have to spell it out for him?

"Swim, mostly," Jake said. "We do some fishing, hiking and we've got mountain bikes. There are some great trails..."

Once again, Vance cut him off. "I'm going back to my cabin," he said. "I didn't think I'd have to join the freakin' Boy Scouts just cause my parents decided they need a holiday from taking care of their kids."

Matt shook his head. He remembered Vance having a bit of an edge the last time they met too. In fact, now that he thought about it, Vance had been the one who had locked him and Jake in one of the sheds on the lodge property as a joke. The two had only been in third grade at the time and had been forced to wait for a couple of hours before Jake's mom finally heard them yelling and pounding on the door and let them out.

"I'll go with you guys," Cody declared, shrugging his bony shoulders and flipping his long hair out of his eyes. "Nothing else to do up here, anyway."

The three boys headed down to the lake, which was perfectly framed by the green of the trees that ringed it. The water was so calm that it was almost a shame to swim in it, Matt thought.

That thought didn't last long, though, as Jake charged past him and thundered into the lake. "First in," he said as he dove and swam a few sharp strokes before resurfacing and shaking the water off his blond curls. "Man, that is refreshing," he yelled.

Matt charged in behind him. He could tell the water was going to be shockingly frigid because even the light spray hitting his legs was numbing. He dove in too, momentarily stunned by the icy rush that hit his forehead. But by the time he came up for air, he felt entirely alive.

Cody was still standing on the shore, idly picking up rocks and tossing them in. "It's too cold, man," he said. "I'm going back up to the lodge."

Matt was secretly happy that Cody was leaving. It was just him and Jake, like he had planned. The two swam for about half an hour, taking turns diving off the platform that was moored near the end of the roped-off swimming area before wading back to the beach.

They flipped down their towels and sat there, taking in the sun. "You ready for Monday?" Matt asked Jake. "North Vale could be pretty tough."

"The question is," Jake said with mock bravado, swinging an imaginary bat out toward the lake, "is North Vale ready for me?"

The boys spent a few more minutes at the beach before the bell began clanging from the main lodge. It must be lunchtime. Jake and Matt scooped up their towels and bolted toward the sound. Swimming and fresh air was enough to make a guy hungry in a hurry.

Jake's mom had whipped up some smokies on the barbecue grill on the deck of the main lodge. Matt had to marvel as he bit into his, which was covered with mustard and hot peppers. It never failed that food tasted better out at Long Lake than it did anywhere else.

For the rest of the afternoon, Matt and Jake tossed around the baseball, took a short hike to the top of the ridge overlooking the lake and helped out Jake's dad by picking several hundred stones off the beach. After a dinner of hamburgers, corn on the cob and baked potatoes, the boys still had a couple of hours before bedtime. Matt felt himself already growing tired, even though it was only eight-thirty. Fresh air usually had that effect on him.

Vance had been silent for most of dinner, but he suddenly pushed his chair back from the table. "I'm goin' down to the lake," he declared, to nobody in particular.

"That's a good idea, Vance," Jake's mom said. "It will be nice down there right now. You guys might even see some fish jumping. Jake, why don't you and the boys go with Vance?"

"Okay, Mom," Jake replied, gathering up his plate and Vance's as well. Jake put the dishes near the sink and motioned to Matt. "Let's go see if the trout are any bigger this year."

The four boys grabbed their jackets and headed down toward the water. The last seconds of twilight were now just fading to black and a big, nearly full, luminous moon had risen over the corner of Long Lake. It was breathtaking, like something out of a movie, Matt thought.

Vance was already a couple hundred feet down the trail, ahead of the other boys. He was stopped, with his hands cupped around his mouth, but Matt could tell what he was doing. He was lighting a cigarette.

"I didn't know you smoked," Jake said casually to his cousin.

Vance said nothing, merely taking a long drag off the cigarette and blowing a stream of smoke in the general direction of the other boys.

"You better not let my dad see you," Jake continued. "He's always worried about forest fires starting out here."

"Your old man should chill," Vance said dismissively. "It's just a smoke, man."

The four boys continued down the path to Long Lake. When they got to the beach, the moon looked even larger than it had at the head of the trail. Its reflection seemed to light up the entire lake, giving the night sky a mystical edge.

Vance and Cody immediately began picking up stones and chucking them into the water. "Watch this," Vance yelled. He threw a rock at the swimming platform, pegging it off the aluminum ladder that Jake and Matt had used to climb out of the water that afternoon.

"Vance, I don't think that's a good idea," Jake said, his voice rising slightly with alarm in a way Matt had never heard it before. "My dad will be pissed if anything gets damaged."

"Jaker, you know what your problem is?" Vance said. "You worry way too much."

Matt had to chuckle to himself. It there was one

thing Jake didn't do it was worry too much. But what kind of idiot threw rocks at something just for the fun of it? No wonder Jake had felt it was necessary to say something to him. Matt would have too.

"You need to chill," Vance continued. "Come on."

Jake and Matt walked slowly over to a log that Vance had plopped down upon. The older boy had pulled something out of the front pocket of his black hoody and was carefully cradling it in his palm. It looked like another cigarette but one that had been squashed so that it wasn't perfectly cylindrical. Now that Matt thought about it, it looked a little like one of those cigarettes that his Uncle Roy always hand-rolled with his own pouch tobacco.

"I don't smoke," Jake said.

"You might want to try this," chuckled Vance. "It's not a cigarette. It's a joint, man. Haven't you ever seen a spliff before? Where do you guys go to school, Timbuktu?"

Matt silently gulped. He had never seen a joint before, and he was pretty sure Jake hadn't either. He knew it was marijuana, but he had never tried it and really didn't have much desire to.

"Course I've seen one before," Jake replied. "Who hasn't?"

Matt was taken aback. Well, for one, he hadn't. Why was Jake pretending that he had?

"Wanna spark it up?" Vance said, eyeing the two of them and Cody.

There was a slight pause as the other three boys stood on the beach in front of the log where Vance was sitting. Matt wanted no part of this. He was trying to figure out what to say when Jake spoke first.

"Sure, man. It's no big deal."

Vance sprung to his feet, plucking a disposable lighter out of his pocket and placing the joint gingerly between his lips. "All righty then," he smiled.

Vance flicked his lighter and held the flame to the end of the joint. A second after it was lit, an oddly sweet odor wafted across the beach. It smelled kind of like the incense Matt's Aunt June sometimes burned in her living room. Matt and Jake watched as the older boy drew heavily on the joint and then held the strange-smelling smoke in his lungs for several seconds before allowing it to escape.

"Now, you," Vance said, motioning to Jake.

Matt watched in astonishment as Jake took the joint from Vance and awkwardly pinched it between his right thumb and index finger. Jake put it to his lips and took a big drag but he couldn't hold it in, coughing and choking as he let out the smoke almost immediately.

"What a rookie!" Vance laughed. Cody seemed to think it was pretty hilarious too.

"Okay, Monster Boy," Vance continued, his harsh eyes moving toward Matt. "It's your turn."

Matt felt frozen. He didn't know how to react. He didn't want to do this, and yet he felt like if he didn't he'd be the laughingstock of the other boys. And he was still reeling from the fact Jake had tried it.

"I gotta go to the bathroom," Matt said suddenly. It was the only way he could think of to get out of this. He turned and bounded up the trail by himself. "Whatever, man," Vance yelled behind him.

Matt walked quickly up the trail toward the lodge. He stopped briefly, looking back at the beach, where Vance, Cody and Jake were still gathered, smoke rising out of the top of their little triangle.

Matt didn't really have to go to the bathroom. But he went all the way up to the lodge door, just the same. When he got there, though, he realized that he couldn't go in. Jake's mom and dad would wonder why he was back there by himself. He couldn't return to the lake, either, or he'd be back in the same situation he just left. Not knowing what else to do, Matt headed out the cabin that he and Jake were to share that night.

The room was dark, but Matt found the light switch and flipped it on. He sat down at the edge of the lower bunk bed on which he had earlier stored his gear. He didn't know what to do next. He pulled out his MP3 player and put on some Sum 41, turning it up nearly full volume.

The music didn't take his mind away from what had just happened. It didn't stop him from feeling awkward, confused and hurt all at the same time. Matt hated himself for having been so nervous when Vance had pulled the joint out of his pocket and at the same time he was shocked that Jake had agreed to try it, like it was no big deal. He and Jake had been best friends since pre-school and not much had ever come between them. But now, sitting alone on his bed in this cabin, Matt felt farther apart from Jake than ever before. It was weird to suddenly feel like maybe he didn't know his friend the way he had always thought he did.

Matt took off his shoes and jacket and lay down on the bed. He pulled his sleeping bag over him and rested his head on the pillow. The stress of the situation had tired him out.

He must have been asleep for at least an hour when he heard somebody fumbling at the cabin door. Matt was groggy but he lifted his head as Jake came into the room. The light was still on, and he caught a glimpse of his friend's face.

"What happened to you, man?" Jake asked. "I thought you were just going to the can. How come you didn't come back?"

"I was just tired," Matt said. It seemed weird to lie

to Jake like this. And at the same time, he knew Jake wouldn't believe him anyway.

"Yeah, I'm going to crash too," Jake replied, flicking off the light switch and heading for the top bunk. "Must be all this fresh air."

Matt felt the bunk beds shake as Jake climbed on top and settled in. Within a few minutes, his friend was snoring. Matt closed his own eyes and tried to go back to sleep, but he couldn't.

It had been a weird night. He felt like something strange had come between him and Jake, and it didn't feel good. It wasn't simply that Jake had tried the joint—Matt knew plenty of kids at South Side smoked pot—it was also the fact that Jake had seemed to choose hanging out with his cousins over Matt. Jake had never made him feel like this before. At the same time, Matt was embarrassed and confused over how he had reacted himself. Should he have tried it too? Jake had seemed pretty normal when he returned. Was there any real harm in what he had done?

Matt shifted his body around, moving the pillow up and down and doubling it in half in an attempt to find a way to get to sleep. He knew it wasn't the bed that was uncomfortable, it was him.

chapter three

"Hey you two sleepyheads! Time to get up." The door to the cabin opened, letting in shards of sunlight and hints of crisp, moist, lake air. It was Jake's mom and she was standing in the doorway wearing an apron and wielding a plastic flipper.

"Pancakes are now on in the main dining hall," she said playfully. "Attention, attention: All campers are requested to report immediately."

Matt rolled out of bed, throwing on his shorts and shoes. Jake was soon on his feet too. "I am starving, Mom," he said.

"Great, there's plenty there," she said. "Wake up Vance and Cody and come on down."

"Come on, Matt," Jake said, grinning at his friend. "Let's go get those losers out of bed."

Matt remembered the previous night. He didn't know how Jake's cousins would react to the way he had left the beach so suddenly without coming back, and he didn't want to find out right at this moment. "You go ahead," he said to Jake. "I want to go brush my teeth and wash up."

Matt still felt strange about the night before. He had never even been offered a joint before, let alone smoked one. He knew Mom wouldn't approve of anything like that. But choosing to avoid it had created a gap between him and Jake, and whether it was real or imagined he definitely felt it.

The four boys wolfed down breakfast and shared jokes at the long wooden table in the common room of the Piancatos' lodge. Matt had been nervous about interacting with Cody and Vance this morning, but neither said anything about the night before and everything seemed pretty normal.

"Matt, your mother asked if I could get you home by noon today," Mr. Piancato said as they finished their breakfast. "That means we've got to get going pretty quick. We'll have to make it a little longer visit next time, okay?"

Matt's older brother, Mark, was coming in from Eton for the day, and his mom wanted some time for the three of them to hang out together. Normally Matt would have been disappointed to leave Long Lake so early on a beautiful spring Sunday. But today was different. He was kind of happy to have an excuse to take off. The night before on the beach had put a damper on the weekend as far as he was concerned.

"Are you going to ride in with us?" Mr. Piancato asked, looking in Jake's direction.

"I don't think so," Jake replied. "Vance and Cody and I are going to take a big hike this afternoon."

Jake's cousins glanced at one another and smiled. "Yeah, we're going to take a huge hike," Vance said.

Matt excused himself from the table and took his dishes to the sink. "I'll go get my stuff together," he said, to nobody in particular.

Mr. Piancato was waiting near the long red station wagon as Matt returned to the main lodge with his knapsack. Jake was on the veranda, and Cody and Vance had gone back to their rooms.

"Well, Matt, it's been great to have you out here again," Mrs. Piancato said, giving him a hug. "You have a nice visit with Mark, and we'll see you again soon."

"Thanks for having me," Matt replied, opening the car door.

"See ya at school," Jake said as Matt climbed in. "Big game tomorrow."

Matt nodded. He put on his seatbelt as Mr. Piancato began to pull the vehicle out of the lodge parking lot. Matt looked out the window as Cody and Vance joined Jake on the veranda. Part of him wanted to stay and go with the three boys on their hike. But another part of him wanted to get home. He didn't particularly like Cody and Vance and he didn't understand why Jake seemed to be choosing them over him.

Matt's mom was in the front yard, planting some perennials in the flower bed by the sidewalk when Mr. Piancato pulled into the driveway. "Thanks a lot," Matt said, jumping out of the station wagon. "That was fun."

Jake's dad waved at Matt's mother and honked his horn as he backed out of the driveway.

"Well, how's my boy?" Mom had risen to her feet with her arms outstretched, waiting to give him a hug with her oversized pink garden gloves.

"Fine," he replied. "It was good to see the lake again. I'm just going to put my stuff away, okay?"

As Matt headed toward the open front door, a blue pickup truck pulled into the driveway and a tall, brown-haired, young man jumped out. Mom held out her arms just as she had for Matt a minute earlier. "Hey, Mark," she beamed. "How's my biggest boy?"

Matt groaned. That was how Mom liked to refer to Mark, his older brother, especially when she hadn't seen him for awhile. Eight years older than Matt, Mark had always been her "biggest boy." And Matt had always been the baby of the family.

"Hey, bro," Mark said, stretching out his right hand to slap Matt's. "What's up? You're getting bigger every time I see you. Still not bigger than me, though."

Matt laughed. Mark was six-foot-three and well defined from daily physical work in the oil fields just outside Eton. Matt was at least seven inches shorter and still developing. Still, the gap between them seemed to be closing a little every time they saw each other.

Mark lived in Eton, a few hours drive away. Nowadays he only came home once every month or so to visit, do his laundry and enjoy some of Mom's cooking. It was always good to see him.

"I just got home too," Matt said. "I was out at the lake with Jaker for the weekend."

"Sweet," said Mark. "How was it?"

"Fun," Matt replied. "I'll tell you about it after I've had a shower."

Matt hustled upstairs to his room to put away his gear and get cleaned up. It was nice to go to the lake but he always enjoyed taking a long, hot shower when he got back.

As he washed his hair, Matt wondered how he should handle the situation with Jake. Would his friend think he was a baby because he hadn't tried the joint? Matt didn't think Jake would be like that, but he wasn't absolutely sure.

Then a thought came to him. Mark was here. It was perfect. He'd probably know how to handle this.

Matt, Mark and Mom spent the day catching up, snacking on crackers, chips, cheese, cold meats and vegetables that she had laid out on the dining room table and playing a lengthy game of Monopoly which, as usual, Mark won. Just before dinnertime, Matt asked Mark if he wanted to go for a walk.

"Sure, Mats," his brother replied. "Let's go check out Anderson Park. I haven't been down there forever."

Matt grabbed his outdoor basketball. "Let's play some ones," he said. "Maybe I'll beat you this time."

"Doubt it," Mark said as the two headed out the door.

It was just a few blocks to Anderson, the park where Matt played most of his outdoor hoops. It was late Sunday afternoon and the court was empty. So he and Mark began a loose game of one-on-one. It wasn't a fair matchup, since Mark was much taller, stronger and older, but the gap between the brothers was closing slowly. Mark sunk a fifteen-foot jumper to end the game, but his winning margin of 11-8 was the closest yet.

"Man, you're getting better—and bigger," Mark said. "Not bad for a seventh-grader."

"Not bad yourself, for an old geezer," Matt laughed.

Now seemed like the perfect time to bring up the situation with Jake. So he just blurted it out. "Hey, Mark, can I ask you something, you know, privately? I don't want Mom to know about this."

"Sure. What's up?"

Matt proceeded to tell his brother all about the previous night, about how Vance had pulled out the joint and about how Jake had smoked it too. He told Mark that he had felt pretty weird and had basically ducked out by saying he had to go to the bathroom.

"What would you have done?" he asked his older brother.

"That's a tough one," Mark admitted. "I probably would have done the same thing you did. You shouldn't get pressured into trying anything you don't want to do. And you're only in the seventh grade. When I was your age, I'd never even heard of a joint."

"I think you were right to stay away from it," Mark continued. "If Jake tried it, that's on him. You have to make up your own mind. Don't let anybody push you into anything."

"But I felt like such a loser," Matt said. "Those other guys probably thought I was a baby."

"Let them think what they want," Mark replied. "You're the one who's got to live with whatever you do or don't do."

The advice made sense to Matt and it made him feel better too. As he and Mark walked down Anderson Crescent on their way to a delicious Sunday roast beef dinner with Mom, Matt found himself feeling quite a bit better about how the weekend had gone.

chapter four

Matt Hill felt excited and nervous on his way to school Monday morning. The thoughts of the lake and what had happened with Jake and his cousins had faded to the background. In the forefront was today's game against the North Vale Nuggets—the first game of the season and the first of his entire middle school baseball career.

In his black equipment bag was his South Side uniform—white button-up baseball jersey with maroon letters spelling out *STINGERS* across the chest, white pants and maroon- and white-striped socks. Matt was also carrying his black three-quarter-cut Easton cleats, his nicely worn-in brown leather Rawlings mitt and his black batting glove.

Matt could see Jake and Phil waiting for him as he approached the big oak at Anderson and Seventh. It was a beautiful, crisp spring morning, an absolutely perfect day for baseball. The three friends walked the rest of the way to South Side together, just as they had almost every day of their first year at the middle school and for several years at Glenview Elementary before that.

At this time of year, it was difficult to concentrate on school. The weather was so nice, all most of the kids could think about was summer and vacation. And Matt was pretty sure most teachers at South Side felt the same way.

That Monday at school dragged a little more than usual for Matt. It seemed that was always the case when he had a big game to look forward to. And this afternoon, his debut as a Stingers varsity baseball team member, was a very big game for sure.

When the 3:35 bell finally rang, Matt eagerly scooped up his backpack and headed for the South Side locker room, which was in one corner of the gymnasium. It was the same locker room that he had used with the Stingers basketball team earlier that school year but now it felt and sounded much different. The squeak of sneakers and the bouncing of balls had been replaced by the sounds of cleats clattering across the tiled floor and aluminum bats clanking in the equipment bags being hauled by Charlie, the Stingers' manager.

Although he had tried on his South Side baseball uniform when he first received it, Matt was excited pulling on his gear for an actual game. He tucked in his jersey and pulled up his baseball socks. He carefully took his maroon South Side ball cap, with the stylized *S* on the front and adjusted it on his head so that it fit just so.

The Stingers were home to North Vale for this game, so they took infield practice first. Matt and an eighth-grader named Kevin Archibald alternated at second base for the warm-up, each fielding sharply hit grounders from Coach Stephens and delivering them on a straight line to Dave Tanner, the Stingers' towering ninth-grade first baseman.

"Take two," Coach Stephens yelled, hitting the ball toward Jake at shortstop.

Jake expertly fielded the grounder, pivoted and flipped the ball to Matt, who was covering second. Matt stepped and threw to first for the double play. It felt good to play with such precision, even if it was just warm-ups.

"Okay, guys, bring it in," Coach Stephens said, calling his team to the dugout. Matt noticed the white lineup board hanging on the wire fence that separated the dugout from the playing field. Written in large capital letters were the starters for South Side. Phil's name was written in at catcher. Jake was the starting shortstop. Matt looked at second, but he already knew what the board would say. Kevin Archibald's name was penciled in at that position rather than his own.

It was disappointing. Matt had started for the varsity basketball team for most of his seventh-grade season, and the Stingers had won the city championship. Now he was merely a bench player. But at the same time, he couldn't blame the coach. Archibald was a pretty decent second baseman and when it came time to bat he wasn't afraid of the ball.

"Okay, everybody knows where they're playing," Coach Stephens barked from the top of the dugout stairs. "I know this is our first game, but I want us to get it right from the start this season. I want to see hustle on and off the field. Run to and from your positions. Pick up the bats and help Charlie out with the equipment. Let's play heads-up baseball when we're on the field and let's get behind our teammates when we're not. Okay?"

Heads nodded all around. The coach moved down into the dugout. He stuck his right hand out in front of his players and they placed theirs on top. "One, two, three! Stingers!" they chanted.

The South Side starters trotted out to the field. Matt watched from his seat in the dugout.

"Hill!" Matt was snapped out of his thoughts by Coach Stephens. "Take this. I want you to score for us when you're not out there. They'll be keeping an official score sheet upstairs, but I want you to keep one for the team. It'll help Charlie put the stats together later."

Matt nodded. But he didn't feel good about this. He hadn't practiced hard every day for the last month to be the stats boy. This is what happens, he thought to himself, when you are scared of the ball.

The self-pity faded as the game began, though. Steve White was on the mound for the Stingers and he had good stuff. He retired the first three North Vale batters without any of them touching the ball. Three strikeouts. White had only thrown two balls.

The South Side players trotted off the field in high spirits. The chatter began in the dugout as Phil started to remove his catching equipment, and Howard Berger, the third baseman with the wide sloping shoulders and close-cropped, flaming red hair, made his way up to the plate.

It wouldn't be easy for South Side to hit in this game, either, as it turned out. Throwing for North Vale was Kenny Lemay, a raw-boned eighth-grader who had starred for the Nuggets in basketball that winter. Lemay wasn't quite as fast as White, the South Side starter, but he had better control. As Coach liked to say, he could "paint the corners."

Howard found that out the hard way, going down swinging in just four Lemay pitches. Next up was Phil, who worked the count to three-and-two but then watched as Lemay found the outside corner for a third strike.

That brought up Jake, with two out and nobody on. Everybody in the South Side dugout leaned forward in anticipation. Matt watched intently with his fingers hooking through the mesh of the dugout fence.

Lemay knew that Jake was the best hitter on the South Side team. They had faced each other several times in Little League games over the years. The North Vale pitcher bore down, and Jake stood in the box, ready for the challenge.

The first pitch was a fastball, slightly inside and high. Jake fouled it off into the left-field stands. Lemay then missed with two balls before coming back with a strike that caught the outside corner.

With the count two-and-two, Lemay opted for the fastball. Jake was ready with a powerful swing. With a loud crack, the line drive shot toward third. But North Vale's third baseman leapt and snagged it in the air. Jake's first at-bat was over and he was out.

Although the Stingers all knew Jake had been unlucky not to hit safely, that at-bat seemed to set the tone for most of the game. Both White and Lemay settled into grooves on the mound and neither let a base runner get past second.

Going into the seventh and final inning, the game was still scoreless. Matt hadn't gotten off the bench, except to keep the score sheet. And nobody else on the South Side squad was exactly tearing it up. Jake had touched Lemay for a pair of singles, but not one other Stinger had hit safely.

"Hill, you're going to second," Coach Stephens said as his team headed out to the field for the top of the last inning. "Take Archibald's place."

Matt grabbed his glove and trotted out to the infield. First baseman Dave Tanner tossed some grounders to him so he could warm up. He fielded them cleanly but still felt nervous as the first North Vale batter came to the plate.

White was still pitching well. He had given up four hits, but hadn't run into any serious trouble during the game. The way the ball zipped into Phil's catching mitt, Matt could tell he was throwing hard despite the fact it was the top of the seventh.

The first North Vale batter got caught looking at a third strike. But the Stingers' ace walked the next man up, leaving a runner on first with ninth-grade standout John Trimble coming to the plate.

Matt remembered Trimble well from basketball too. He had been a talented guard on the North Vale team that had played South Side in the city championship game. He was also an outstanding shortstop and a good hitter. The Stingers were in trouble with him at the plate.

Matt readied himself as White reared back to deliver the first pitch against Trimble. It was another fastball, but the Nugget infielder was primed for it. The ball leapt off his bat, heading straight for Matt in the gap between first and second. Matt lunged for the baseball, stabbing it backhanded with his glove. Instinctively he flipped the ball to second base where Jake was covering. Jake relayed the ball to Tanner at first. It was a double play, just like they had worked on in warm-ups.

The Stingers cheered as they headed for the dugout with the last bat to come and still no score. Matt felt warm inside. He had made a nice catch and started the double play. It felt good to do something right for a change.

Matt glanced at the batting order in the dugout. Jake was up first, followed by Tanner and then him. He would have to face Lemay, who looked at least as fast as White. Matt's heart raced on the bench. Part of him wanted to step in there and smack the ball. But he knew another part of him was afraid.

"Stewart," Coach Stephens called, motioning for Paul Stewart, a squat muscular ninth-grader who hadn't been in the game yet. "You're going to bat in Hill's spot."

Matt was stunned. He hadn't even got to the plate and coach was already pinch-hitting for him. This was embarrassing. But somehow, Matt also realized that he probably would have done the same thing in the coach's position. Matt had been hitting awful against fast pitchers throughout practice sessions. The game was on the line, and Coach didn't want to let it slip away.

As Lemay took his warm-up pitches on the North Vale mound, Coach Stephens motioned for Matt to come talk to him in the corner of the dugout. "Don't take this the wrong way, Matt," he said gently. "I put you in the top of the seventh for your defense and you did great. That was a tough catch and a nice double play. But Paul's been hitting better against the fast stuff. Don't worry, we can work on your hitting in practice."

"Sure, Coach," Matt said, managing a weak smile. Maybe it was better to be pinch-hit for rather than have everybody in the park discover he was afraid of the ball.

Jake was the first batter of the inning. He stood in strong against Lemay, ripping a two-one pitch into right-center field. The Stingers had the winning run on base with nobody out and Dave Tanner, one of their best hitters, at the plate.

Lemay knew the game was on the line or maybe he was trying too hard to throw the perfect pitch. Whatever the reason, the North Vale chucker grooved a medium-speed offering right down the middle of the plate. Tanner jumped all over it, lifting a high fly ball all the way to the fence in right field. The ball bounced off the white wooden boards and

rebounded wildly into right field where the Nuggets'
fielder tried to chase it down.

Meanwhile, Jake was on the dead run. He rounded
second and headed for third with so much speed that
a slide wasn't necessary. The throw came in from
right field, but it was well over the third baseman's
head. Jake sped home. South Side had won its first
game of the season one to nothing.

Cheers erupted in the stands and in the dugout as
the Stingers high-fived each other. Matt felt himself
caught up in the emotion, the thrill of the win taking
the sting out of the fact Coach had been so eager to
pinch-hit for him.

Coach Stephens was busy congratulating his players after the game, speaking with each one individu-
ally. He came over to Matt and patted him on the
back. "Nice job in the field," he said quietly.

"I guess I need work on my hitting," Matt replied.
He felt stupid the moment he said it. But he couldn't
stop dwelling on the fact that Coach hadn't shown
any faith in him as a batter.

"Look, Matt," Coach Stephens said patiently.
"Everybody has some phase of his game that needs
work. And that's what we're going to do with you at
the plate."

Matt looked at him quizzically.

"Can you take some extra batting practice on
Saturdays?" Coach Stephens asked.

Matt didn't see why not. "Sure, Coach."

"Good, then. Come out Saturday morning at, say, 9:30. Meet Charlie at the door to the locker room and he'll let you in."

Charlie? Matt wondered why he would be there. Just then, Coach cleared his throat and called his players together in the locker room.

"All right people," he said, making sure everybody was listening. "Nice game out there today, especially for your first of the season. There's plenty of room for improvement, but I think we can be solid this year. Nice pitching, Whitey."

Steve White grinned from ear to ear. He had thrown a great game and he knew it.

"Hit the showers," the coach continued. "We'll take tomorrow off and practice here Wednesday. Be ready to work."

chapter five

The posters seemed to be plastered across every wall and bulletin board in South Side Middle School. *Spring Fling. Who Will You Bring?* one of them read.

Matt stared at the sign for a couple of seconds. It took that long to register just what the sign meant. *Who Will You Bring?* As in *Who is your date?*

Matt gulped. He hadn't thought about asking a girl to any dance. In fact, he hadn't thought that much about girls, period. For one thing, he had been preoccupied with sports since school began the previous fall. First it was basketball, now baseball. And if he wasn't practicing or playing, there was a ton of schoolwork to do. Middle school meant more choices and freedom than he and his friends had enjoyed at Glenview Elementary. But it also meant more responsibility and much tougher subject matter. For the first time in his life, Matt had homework pretty much every night.

He didn't know exactly what to make of this Spring Fling that was coming up at the school on June 5. He and his friends hadn't talked about it at all.

"Checkin' out the big dance?" came a voice from behind. It was Amar Sunir, another of Matt's long-time friends. Amar didn't play baseball—his family was into soccer and cricket when it came to out-door, summer sports—so he and Matt hadn't seen each other as much lately as they did through the basketball season, when Amar was a fellow starter on the Stingers.

"You going?" Matt asked.

"I guess so," Amar replied. "I mean, if everybody else is, I will."

"Do we have to bring somebody?" Matt emphasized the word "bring" like it carried some unfathomable ramifications.

"Nah," Amar said. "I don't think so. It's just a sort of a hang-out thing with good tunes."

"I'll probably go," Matt said, eyeing the poster one last time.

The two headed into Room 107 where they shared morning advisory period with Miss Dawson. South Side Middle School students began each day with a twenty-minute period run by their advisory teacher, whose responsibility it was to help shepherd a group of twenty-five students through their school year. Matt felt lucky to have Miss Dawson, a tall woman with long dark hair and hazel eyes, as his adviser. She was one of the coolest teachers in the school, and she seemed to understand even the weirdest problems her students were experiencing. Having Miss Dawson to bounce questions off and to talk with had helped make the transition from elementary to middle school easier than it might have been.

As they took their seats, Matt spied Andrea Thomas sitting in her usual spot two rows over. The blond-haired, blue-eyed seventh-grader with the long legs smiled at him, and he blushed in return—he didn't know why. Matt gave her a little half-wave in reply, hoping not too many kids had noticed.

Something was different about Andrea today, though, and Matt couldn't quite put his finger on it. Then it came to him in a flash. "Hey, you got your cast off," he exclaimed, loud enough for most of the class to hear and setting off giggles among the girls seated around Andrea.

"Yeah, I was away from school yesterday getting it cut off. It healed up great and the doctors say I can start practicing with the softball team right away," Andrea said.

Matt was pleased she was going to be able to play sports again soon. She was a terrific athlete who had injured her leg in a soccer collision last fall, just two games into the regular season for South Side. Andrea had spent the winter in a cumbersome red cast that had run from her foot to her thigh. But she had put her time to good use, working as the manager-trainer for the boys' basketball team and helping Matt through some injuries of his own.

"We've got a game today, you know," Andrea said to Matt. "We're playing North Vale. You going to come cheer us on?"

Matt felt his cheeks redden. He noticed Amar looking at him strangely. "Yeah, maybe," he said coolly. "If I can."

Matt turned and faced the front of the class. Miss Dawson was about to begin, but Matt's mind was somewhere else. Why had Andrea just asked him to come out to the girls' softball game? Part of him was happy that she had. He liked Andrea and had felt from almost the first time they met that she was easier to talk to than other girls. He wanted to go to watch the softball game, as long as his friends wouldn't think it was some kind of date or something.

The rest of the day flew by. As students were being dismissed from their last class, Principal Walker reminded them over the loudspeaker system: "Our own Stingers girls' softball team plays its first game today. Come on out and support them."

Matt had forgotten about the game, but since there was no boys' baseball practice, he was free to go. He leaned over to Phil and asked, "You want to go check out the second-best ball team in school?"

"Yeah, sure," Phil said. "I can go for awhile. Then I've got to get to Grandma's store."

Phil was the most responsible hard-working kid Matt had ever known. Not only was he a straight-A student and a varsity baseball and basketball player, but he was also a chess whiz. To top everything off, he worked several hours a week in Wong's Grocery, a family corner store located not far from the school and run by his aging grandmother.

Of all the things he was good at, baseball was probably Phil's forte. He had consistently been the top catcher through Little League, always able to block any pitch and possessing a gun of a right arm that was capable of throwing out runners at any base. Best of all, Phil had a mind for baseball. Coach Stephens liked the fact that he was always thinking one play ahead of everybody else.

Matt and Phil sat in the bleachers behind the home plate fence for the softball game. It was South Side's first game of the season and, like the boys, they were facing North Vale. But unlike the game the day before, the Nuggets girls' team wasn't very good. The game wasn't close and it was called after just four innings with the Stingers leading 21-2.

Matt and Phil were heading past the dugouts when they saw Andrea coming toward them. She was still limping slightly but moving much faster than she had all winter. "Hey guys," she said. "Thanks for coming out."

Matt felt his ears growing hot. "You guys are pretty good," he said, fumbling for something to say. "I mean, you girls are."

Andrea laughed. Matt waved self-consciously, and he and Phil continued walking toward Wong's Grocery.

"You going to the dance?" Phil asked his friend, after they had walked a ways in silence.

"I guess so. I mean, why not?"

"You should ask Andrea to go," Phil said matter-of-factly.

"Andrea? Are you serious?" Matt was taken aback. He knew he liked her, but he didn't realize anybody else could tell.

"For sure," Phil said. "She's pretty cool. And she obviously likes you too."

Matt felt himself getting embarrassed all over again. "Yeah, right," he said, trying to muster up some sarcasm. "Why don't you ask her, Philly?"

Matt was trying to do anything to turn the conversation in another direction. He wasn't sure why, but talking about asking out a girl made him nervous, even with a long-time friend. Maybe especially with a friend.

They had reached Wong's Grocery, the tiny, old, white corner store that had served the neighborhood for more than thirty years. "I gotta go," Phil said. "But I'm serious, you should ask her."

"Whatever," Matt said. "What do you think I am, some kind of bossa nova or something?"

Phil broke into a huge belly laugh. "I think you mean Casanova, don't you?"

chapter six

Matt was jarred awake by the obnoxious alarm of his bedside clock radio. It was 9:15 AM on Saturday, and he had been sleeping for ten hours. But still he felt groggy.

No time to dawdle, though. This was the morning Coach Stephens had asked him to report for extra batting practice. Matt didn't know what good taking more swings was going to do. His problem wasn't hitting. It was being able to stand in there when the ball was coming at high speeds.

It wasn't like Matt was afraid of getting hurt, at least no more afraid than anybody else his age. He had taken plenty of elbows in basketball and hard tackles in soccer. It was different with a baseball, though. Something about a small, hard ball coming at him in such unpredictable fashion out of a pitcher's hand was scary. He wasn't afraid of charging a hard grounder, and he had even taken a couple of those in the face. But when a tall fourteen-year-old kid with sinewy arms was winding up to throw, Matt couldn't resist the urge to jump back. And like Coach said, it was pretty hard to take a decent swing at the baseball when you were jumping away from it.

After wolfing down some toast and orange juice for breakfast, Matt threw on a sweatshirt, his maroon Stingers cap and some sweatpants, hopped on his bike and pedaled the six blocks to South Side Middle School. The campus was empty, and Matt hoped he had got the day right because there was no sign of Coach Stephens' car. He wheeled around back by the locker room door. Charlie was there, waiting with an equipment bag and a set of keys.

"Where's Coach?" Matt asked.

"Can't make it today," Charlie replied. "He told me to help you out."

Matt was irritated. He looked at Charlie, with his huge leg brace and his ever-present limp. The manager's disability prevented him from running at even quarter-speed. That kept Charlie from playing any sports competitively. So how, exactly, was he going to help out Matt?

"Maybe we should just wait for a day when Coach can be here," Matt said, eying Charlie.

"Nope," the manager replied, shaking his head back and forth. "We've got everything we need, and

Coach told me what drills to run. I didn't waste my Saturday morning so you could just go home. Let's get started."

Charlie's serious manner took Matt by surprise. "Okay," Matt said. "What do we do, then?"

Charlie found the key that opened the locker room door and headed over to the equipment storage area. "Come over and give me a hand," he said. It wasn't so much a request as a command, Matt thought to himself.

"We're going to take the pitching machine out to the field," Charlie said. "You grab that end."

Matt and Charlie wheeled the machine out the locker room door and down the path to the empty baseball field. They set it up on the mound and, using a yellow extension cord, plugged it into a power outlet in the home dugout.

"You know how to work this thing?" Matt asked.

"Sure," Charlie replied with a confident grin. "It's not exactly rocket science. You go back to the locker room and get the bag of soft practice balls. I'll get it going."

Matt returned with the black bag filled with at least fifty yellow balls. They were shaped like a baseball but made out of a soft synthetic material that didn't hurt half as hard if they hit you.

"We'll use these today," Charlie said. "Maybe next time, we'll use real baseballs."

Next time? Matt was wondering what he had got himself into. It was kind of embarrassing being out here on a Saturday, taking orders from a student manager. What would his teammates say about it? They already thought he was enough of a wuss being afraid of the baseball.

Charlie had the pitching machine whirring, the wheel turning and spitting out balls toward the plate as the manager fed them through the top of the apparatus. He was busy adjusting the height and speed so that the ball would come across the plate every time.

"We're going to start at forty miles an hour," Charlie said. "Grab a bat and we'll try a few."

Matt settled in on the right side of the plate. Charlie began feeding balls into the machine. The balls came across the plate in roughly the same spot every time, right across the heart. Matt was taking healthy cuts, hitting at least three out of five pitches, most of them to the outfield. He was beginning to feel warmed up.

"Okay, that's enough," Charlie said. "Now comes the fun part."

Matt had no idea what Charlie meant. He stood back from the plate as the manager bent over the side of the machine and adjusted it. Suddenly the ball was coming across the plate, but high and inside, just the kind of pitches that scared the daylights out of Matt.

"Go ahead, get in your stance," Charlie said. Matt complied, lining up slightly farther away from the plate than he had before.

"Get closer," Charlie said. "You can't hit from the warm-up circle."

Matt felt a twitch of anger. Charlie was now making jokes at his expense. The manager, who didn't even play the game. Nice.

"Okay, Matt," Charlie continued. "I just want you to stand there for about twenty pitches. Don't move back at all, unless you think the ball is going to hit you."

Matt nodded. He stood inside the batter's box as Charlie began dropping balls into the top of the machine. They were whizzing within six inches of his batting helmet. Initially he flinched and moved backward. But over the last ten pitches, Matt stood his ground.

"I'm going to turn up the speed now," Charlie said. The balls began whirring faster past his batting helmet. It was more difficult to stay in there and Matt felt himself instinctively sliding backward a couple of times. But for the most part, he stayed in the box.

"Good stuff," Charlie said, looking impressed. "Now comes the tough part. This machine has an alternate switch on it. I'm going to set it up for a strike, a ball inside high and a ball inside low. Then I'm going to mix them up. I want you to hit the good pitches and leave the bad ones, okay? But don't jump out of the box unless you think it's going to hit you."

Matt stepped back in the batter's box. The first pitch was clearly a ball, low and inside. He left it alone. The second was a strike and he took a cut at it, hitting it foul. The third pitch was high and inside and he couldn't help himself. He jumped back from the plate.

"Come on, Matt," Charlie exclaimed. "It's only going fifty and it's a soft ball. It's not going to hurt you even if it does hit you."

Matt was burning inside again. What did Charlie know about anything? When had he ever played ball? Matt focused again and stepped back into the box. He would show Charlie.

Matt gradually began making the right decision on almost every pitch. Charlie put up his hand. "Last drill for today," he said authoritatively. "I'm turning up the speed to seventy."

Matt realized it would get tougher, but he jumped back in the box. After struggling through the first few pitches adjusting to the higher speed, he began to relax and find the groove again. Soon he was standing in there and not swinging at the faster, inside pitches. And he was smacking the ball into the outfield on the strikes.

"That's enough for today," Charlie barked. "Good job, Hill."

Matt glanced at the clock on the outside of the school. It was already noon. He had been taking batting practice for two hours. He was sweating heavily from all the swings.

"We'll do this again next week, okay?" Charlie said. "We'll have you hitting like A-Rod in no time."

Matt groaned inside. Charlie was doing his best Coach Stephens impersonation. It made him feel a little funny taking orders from a manager. But at the same time, Matt had to admit that Charlie seemed to know a thing or two about batting. A couple of tips he had given Matt about his swing had been bang-on. And it was nice of the manager to give up his Saturday morning to help him out. After all, it wasn't Charlie who was afraid of the ball.

"Thanks, Chucky," Matt said, using the nickname many of the players substituted for the manager's real name.

"Can you just call me Charlie, or even Charles?" he replied. "I hate Chucky. It makes me think of that puppet from those horror flicks."

Matt and Charlie shared a laugh. Then they wheeled the pitching machine back into the locker room and stored the practice balls away.

"Thanks, man," Matt said, giving Charlie a high five.

Matt noticed a satisfied look in the manager's eyes.

"No problem," Charlie said. "It's all about helping the team, right?"

chapter seven

Matt and his mom were just sitting down to Sunday dinner of baked ham, roast potatoes and corn on the cob when the phone rang. "Let the machine get it," Mom said. Too late, Matt had already picked up.

"Mattster." The bubbly voice was unmistakably Jake. "What's up?"

Matt explained that he was just about to eat dinner. "I'll call you back, okay?" he said. He returned to the table a little happier than when he had picked up the phone. Since that weird night at Long Lake, he hadn't felt quite as close to Jake. It was good to hear from him, whatever he wanted to talk about.

"It was just Jake," Matt said. "I'll call him back."

It was just the two of them for dinner tonight. Mark had visited the previous weekend and he was coming home only once a month or so now. But that was all right with Matt. He enjoyed the occasional quiet dinner with his mom. The weeks were so hectic with school, sports and Mom's job as a real estate agent that it was nice to be able to catch up.

Unlike some kids, Matt kind of enjoyed spending time with his mother. Sure, she could be pretty hokey at times, but they had plenty of laughs together and he always knew she wanted what was best for him. That never failed to come across, no matter how mad she got at him for not cleaning up his room, doing the dishes or for stalling on his homework.

"I see from your school newsletter that you have a dance coming up," she said. "Are you planning to go?"

"I don't know. I guess. But I can't figure out if we're supposed to take someone. You know, like a date?" Just the word "date" seemed forced and a bit silly to Matt.

"I don't think you have to, Matt," Mom said, her lips slipping into a half grin. "Is there somebody you were thinking of taking?"

"Naw, not really," Matt said before quickly changing the subject. "We've got a game tomorrow. Are you coming?"

"I'll try to make it but I've got a house to show in the afternoon. What time does it start?"

"Right at 4:30," he said. "We're playing Manning. I don't think they're very good."

Matt went on to offer his analysis of the entire South Side baseball team to his mother, player by player. She listened intently. Matt knew it wasn't because she was a huge baseball fan—in fact, she barely knew the rules—but she was interested in whatever he was doing.

They were just finishing dessert, an apple pie that Mom had baked the previous fall and frozen, when the phone rang again. Matt jumped up to grab it. It was practically a reflex action.

"Sorry, man." It was Jake again. "Can you talk?"

Matt took the portable phone upstairs to his room. He closed his door, stretched out on his bed and looked out the window as dusk was settling in on Anderson Crescent. "What's up, Jake?"

"I've got an idea," Jake said hesitantly. "It's about the dance."

Matt waited for Jake to continue.

"I kind of want to ask Marcia," he said.

"You mean Marcia Evans? You want to take her to the dance?"

"I don't know about *taking* her," Jake said. "Maybe just meeting her there and hanging out. You know, more casual. Not like it's an official date or anything."

Matt chuckled to himself. Not like a date? This was exactly like a date. Jake just didn't want to use the word. But Matt couldn't really blame him. This was brand-new territory for both of them.

"So, I was wondering," Jake continued. "Marcia is like best friends with Andrea, you know. And you and Andrea get along pretty good..."

Matt could tell where Jake was going with this one. "Why do you say that?" he asked defensively.

"It's pretty obvious, dude. I mean, I heard she asked you to watch the softball game the other day."

Matt blushed. He was glad nobody could see him.

"She's all right," Matt said. "I mean, she's pretty cool. We could hang out. If she wants to, that is."

"Awesome," Jake said. "Let me talk to Marcia and I'll set it up. Okay?"

"All right," Matt replied. "Later."

As Matt hung up, he felt a strange mix of nerves and excitement.

The next morning, only Phil was waiting under the oak tree on Anderson Crescent. He and Matt hung around for a couple of minutes to see if Jake would show up. He didn't. "We'd better go or we'll be late," Phil said, eyeing his watch.

They walked the rest of the way to school together. By the time they arrived at South Side, the bell was about to ring. Matt strolled down the hallway to his locker, which was just outside Room 107, where they took morning advisory.

He was pulling out his books for the first few classes of the day when he heard a voice behind him. "Hi, Matt." He turned around to see Andrea standing there. She smiled.

"Jake said you guys are going to the dance on Friday," Andrea said matter-of-factly. "So, are we all going to hang out there?"

"I guess so," Matt stammered, feeling his throat tighten and his voice rise slightly. "I mean, yeah, if that's good with you."

"Okay," Andrea replied. She turned around and headed into class without another word. That was weird, Matt thought.

As he entered class, he noticed Andrea talking to two or three other girls, including Marcia Evans. They were smiling and whispering. They all looked at him while he hurriedly found his desk.

The second bell rang and Miss Dawson began her advisory session. Every morning she would use the twenty-minute period to answer questions students had about middle school. But she always began the session with a two- or three-minute talk that carried a theme. Today's theme was "Making Responsible Choices." Matt barely heard a word she said. All he kept thinking was that he had just agreed to a date. He was going to his first school dance and he was taking a girl. Well, maybe not taking her, but meeting her there and hanging out together. What would Phil and Amar say? What about the guys on the team? What would he wear? It might have been the first time in his life that he had thought much at all about what he was going to wear.

chapter eight

As Matt headed into the dugout, he looked up into the stands behind the third-base line. There was his mom, sitting beside Mrs. Piancato and Phil's grandmother. She had made it to the game after all.

Once on the bench, he waited for Coach Stephens to put the lineup card on the fence. Coach never told anybody except the pitcher and catcher who was playing where until the lineup card went up. That way, everybody warmed up as if he was starting. With his mom in the stands, Matt said a silent prayer, wishing his name would be on that list. But when Coach Stephens hung the lineup card, Kevin Archibald's name was written in at second base. Matt would be starting the game on the bench.

"Here you go." Charlie handed Matt the clipboard with the game sheet. He was going to be keeping stats again. Once again, Matt bristled. He wasn't in a South Side uniform just so he could be a manager.

The Manning Minutemen did not have a good team this year and were no match for the Stingers. That much was obvious from the first at-bat, when South Side third baseman Howard Berger ripped a pitch into right field and it rolled all the way to the fence. By the time the Manning fielder had reached the ball, Berger was already on third.

Next up was Phil, who walked on just four pitches. That brought Jake to the plate. With two balls and no strikes, Jake hammered the next pitch to deep center field. Howard and Phil scored easily, and Jake was standing up at second with a huge grin on his face. The rout was on.

By the time the top of the fifth came, the Stingers had a 10-0 lead and it was no longer a competitive game. Matt had immersed himself in the detailed process of keeping stats. "Hill, you're going in at second for Archibald," Coach said. Matt handed the clipboard to Kevin, grabbed his glove and ran out to second.

Although he tried to be casual about it, Matt stole a glance into the stands and waited for his mom to realize that he was finally in the game. A smile broke out over her face and she waved at him. "Let's go, Mats!" she yelled.

Matt lowered his head. It was the nickname his mom liked to use whenever she was excited but it was kind of embarrassing. He had become "Mats"

while he was in kindergarten. He had begun sign-
ing his name that way because he was a huge fan of
the Toronto Maple Leafs' captain Mats Sundin. The
name had stuck.

Manning was such a weak team that Matt didn't
get a single ball hit to him at second base. In fact,
nobody was touching anything being thrown by
Andrew McTavish, who was likely the second best
pitcher on the South Side team behind Steve White.

Meanwhile, the Stingers continued to roll on the
offensive side of the game. Matt got his first at-bat in
the bottom of the fifth, taking four straight balls as
Manning's starting pitcher faded fast. He managed
to score too, when McTavish drove him home with a
sharp single to right.

In the bottom of the sixth, Manning's coach
called a time-out. He walked to the mound to talk
to his pitcher. The two spoke briefly before the lanky
pitcher lowered his head, put the ball in the coach's
hand and walked slowly into the dugout.

Seconds later, a towering replacement trotted out
toward the mound. Matt recognized this kid. It was
Kenny Forshaw. Forshaw stood at least six-foot-five
and had been a terrific post player for Manning's
basketball team. But he had never seen Forshaw play
baseball, let alone pitch.

The plate umpire gave Forshaw his warm-up pitches
and Matt couldn't help but think the kid needed

them. The Manning reliever resembled a gigantic, gangly spider as he uncoiled from his windup. He was throwing smoke, but he was all over the place. High one pitch, low the next, inside, outside. Everywhere but over the plate.

Matt watched as Jake battled Forshaw at the plate. The Manning pitcher was giving his buddy nothing decent to hit but Jake was showing a good, patient eye. The count was three and one as Forshaw wound up and delivered a fastball, this time down the middle. Jake swung, but he was a fraction late getting around on the blur of a pitch, lifting a high foul down the right field line. The Minuteman fielder chased it down, putting Jake out for the first time that day. Manning's dugout, silent until now, exploded in cheers.

Dave Tanner was next up, but he didn't fare any better. It seemed to Matt that he wasn't standing in there quite as confidently as usual. Who could blame him? Forshaw was getting faster, and wilder, with every pitch. Tanner went down, swinging weakly at a ball that was well outside and high.

Matt gulped. He was next up. As he walked toward the plate, he thought his knees would give out. This kid was throwing so fast. What if he got hit?

The first pitch whizzed downward from Forshaw's hand and ended up somewhere around Matt's ankles. He managed to hold his ground and resisted the urge to swing. It was a ball. He was ahead in the count.

Forshaw wound up again. The ball catapulted toward Matt. All Matt could tell was that it was headed inside. He ducked backward so quickly that he fell to the ground. The kids in the Manning dugout laughed. Matt got up, shaking himself off. Afraid of the ball, he thought to himself. Everybody else must be thinking the same thing.

Matt was determined to stand in there this time. Forshaw delivered another hard pitch inside. Matt swung, as much to protect himself as anything else. He connected weakly, sending the ball foul down the right field line. "Make him pitch to you, Matt," came Coach's voice from the dugout.

Forshaw wound up again, this time delivering a perfect strike that split the heart of the plate. Matt swung but missed badly. He knew why too. As the ball had been delivered, he had rocked backward away from the pitch. You can't hit it if you're ducking away, he told himself.

The count was 2 and 2. Matt felt the pressure building. Forshaw was winding up again. This time the ball was well outside. Matt left it alone. Full count.

The Manning pitcher stalled for a second on the mound, kicking the dirt by the pitching rubber and staring intently at the plate. Matt gripped his bat tighter, waiting for the deciding pitch. It was coming now, faster than all the others. Matt couldn't help himself, he ducked back again, though not as far as before. The pitch caught the top corner.

"Strike three!" yelled the umpire. On the mound, Forshaw cocked his arm and pumped his fist. It was as if Manning had won the World Series.

Matt headed back to the dugout. He snuck a peek into the stands at his mom. She was clapping hard, yelling, "It's okay, Matty." Matt didn't feel like it was okay, though. He had struck out ducking again.

Charlie met him at the dugout steps, handing him his glove and hat and taking his batting helmet. "Much better, Matt," he said. "You stayed in there for most of that at-bat, even got a piece of Forshaw. He's fast, man."

The words made Matt feel a little better—even if they were coming from the manager. And none of the players in the South Side dugout seemed to be making fun of him this time. He guessed everybody, even Jake, was a little intimidated by Forshaw.

Manning went one-two-three in its half of the seventh and the game was over. South Side had won 12-0 and was a perfect two wins and no losses on the season.

"Good work out there," Coach Stephens told his players in the dugout afterward. "I saw some improvement on the field, and Mac threw a good solid seven for us. We'll see you Wednesday for practice."

Matt's mom had a late house showing that night so she suggested they go out for a pizza first. Matt didn't need his arm twisted on this one. They headed to Classico's, the neighborhood restaurant that they always ordered from. They grabbed a booth at the back and ordered up a medium double-cheese, double-pepperoni and onions—the family favorite—and two large Cokes.

"You boys had a good game today," his mom said.

"Yeah, it wasn't bad," Matt replied. "I still can't hit, though."

"Don't worry. It'll come. That kid at the end was throwing pretty fast. I don't blame you for being a little nervous."

A little nervous? Oh, man, now even his own mother knew he was afraid of the ball.

"By the way," she said. "How did your practice on Saturday go? Weren't you working on hitting with Coach Stephens then?"

"Yeah, I was working on hitting, but not with Coach," Matt replied. "It was just me and Chuck...I mean, Charlie."

"Is that your manager? The boy with the big leg brace?"

Matt, who had a too-big bite of pizza in his mouth, nodded.

"Why does he wear that brace, Matt?" his mom asked. "Is it permanent?"

That was a good question. Matt knew Charlie had some sort of early childhood disease that had left him with a leg problem. But he didn't know what the disease was or whether Charlie would have to wear the brace forever.

"That's nice of him to come out and help you on a Saturday," his mom said.

Matt hadn't thought much about it before. But Charlie had come out on a Saturday morning. And it wasn't like he was getting anything out of it himself.

"Yeah," Matt found himself saying. "He's a good guy."

chapter nine

Friday came sooner than Matt wanted it to. "Don't forget the big Spring Fling tonight at 7:00 PM," Principal Walker reminded students during the afternoon announcements.

The dance had even affected baseball. Because of it, Coach Stephens had cancelled practice this afternoon. Matt had arranged to meet Phil and Jake before the dance, but first he had to head home and get ready.

After taking a shower, he picked out what he thought were his coolest jeans and then tried to decide what shirt to wear. He settled on a loose-fitting khaki button-up with a white T-shirt underneath. Over top, he wore the plain gold chain his mother had given him for his birthday. It was the first time he had ever worn it.

Mom was still out showing houses to clients, but she had left Matt a note on the stove. *There's pasta and salad in the fridge*, it read. *Have a great time at the dance and call me if you need a ride.*

Matt didn't feel much like eating. The insides of his stomach were flipping about and he felt on edge. He and Jake were meeting Andrea and Marcia at the dance. It was supposed to be pretty casual, and it wasn't like they had to pick up the girls and meet their parents and all that stuff. But still, it was different. They had actually made plans to all hang out together.

It was 6:30 when Matt slipped out the front door, carrying his jacket. In just a few minutes he was at the oak tree on Anderson, where Phil was waiting.

"No Jake?" Matt asked.

"He called me and said his parents would drop him off here," Phil said. "They were running late."

It was just a couple of minutes before the Piancatos' red station wagon pulled up alongside them. But one look at the car and Matt's spirits fell. Not only was Jake in the backseat, but so were his cousins, Cody and Vance. What were those guys doing here? Matt thought. They didn't even go to South Side.

"Hey guys! Sorry we're late," Jake burst out of the car. "Cody and Vance are going to hang with us tonight too. Their dad got sent to this conference in San Francisco, and they are staying with us for the weekend."

"Hey," Matt said, eyeing the cousins warily.

"Hey," Cody replied. Vance simply nodded his head coolly.

The five boys headed down Anderson toward South Side. The school parking lot was full of cars dropping kids off, and Matt could hear the sounds of Fifty Cent coming from inside. This was kind of cool, he thought. There had been dances at Glenview Elementary, but they had always been in the afternoon with all the lights on. This was different.

Each of the boys got his hand stamped by Principal Walker as he entered the building. The principal gave Cody and Vance the once-over, wondering who they were before Jake piped up. "Mr. Walker, these are my cousins from Eton," he said. "They're just here for the weekend."

The principal stamped both boys' hands and ushered them in. The gym was dark except for the light show that had been set up by the DJ. Red, yellow, blue and orange lights flashed on and off in synch with the music, while a strobe light at the front seemed to freeze the dancers in mid-stride every time it flashed. The bass was pumping out of the giant speakers set up at the front of the gym. The place where Matt and his buddies had sweated it out for countless basketball practices had taken on a completely different feel.

Jake spied them first: a small cluster of girls standing in the corner near the concession stand. There was Marcia, dressed in tight jeans and a white sweater, along with her friends Kate and Simone. And there was Andrea.

Matt was used to seeing Andrea in gym shorts or sweats. For half the time he had known her, her right leg had been in a huge red cast. But she looked so much different tonight. A short black dress, nylons and dress shoes made her look so grown up. So...Matt didn't know how to describe it in his mind. So beautiful, maybe?

Andrea's big blue eyes lit up as she saw him coming. She waved. As Matt drew closer, the difference in Andrea was even more stunning. Her long blond hair was styled differently tonight and she was wearing makeup.

"Hey," he said. He realized he didn't have the faintest idea how to act.

"Hey," Andrea said. "You look really nice tonight."

Embarrassed, he said, "Um, thanks." He knew he should tell her she looked great too, but the words wouldn't come. "The gym sure looks different. Guess you're not taping any ankles or knuckles tonight."

They both laughed. Andrea had been a terrific student manager-trainer for the boys' basketball team that winter. And she had taped up Matt on a couple of occasions.

With small talk out of the way, Matt began to feel more comfortable. He stood by Andrea and the two watched the dancers together. He felt like he should ask her to dance, but he also felt like he didn't know how. To dance, that is.

"Let's go," she said, arching her eyebrows at Matt. "This is a good song!"

Matt followed Andrea out onto the dance floor. There was a first time for everything, he guessed. Andrea was already moving to the music, a smile across her face. She looked comfortable on the dance floor despite recovering from a leg injury. Matt, on the other hand, felt like a complete geek. He imagined all the movies he had seen of people dancing in night-clubs and tried to remember what they had done. He could fake it as well as the next guy, he thought.

As the evening wore on, Matt felt more and more at ease. It was too loud to talk inside the gym so he was off the hook as far as making conversation with Andrea went. And she seemed quite content just standing beside him, grooving to the music and dancing to the occasional song.

About an hour into the dance, Jake leaned close to Matt and whispered. "I'm going outside with Cody and Vance," he said. "You coming?"

Matt shook his head. Why would those guys want to go outside? The dance was in here. He noticed Marcia Evans was leaving with the other boys.

"Where are they going?" Andrea asked Matt.

"Just outside," he said.

They shrugged at each other and laughed. Andrea moved a little closer to Matt and he didn't move away. Her shoulder was touching his.

A couple minutes later, Marcia came back into the gym. She was by herself and she didn't look happy. "Can I talk to you?" she asked Andrea, pointing to the washroom. "In there."

Marcia and Andrea left Matt by himself on the edge of the dance floor. By now, it was full for practically every song—a combination of the song selection getting better and everybody's nerves easing.

When the girls returned five minutes later, Matt leaned over to Andrea. He could smell the light perfume she was wearing. "What's up?" he asked.

"I'll tell you later," she promised, easing back into her position just in front of Matt, watching the dance floor.

An hour later, the music stopped and Principal Walker came to the center of the gym with a microphone. "I'd like to thank the Spring Fling committee and all the teachers and parents for putting this dance on," he said. "This is the last song, so enjoy it and thanks for coming."

It was a slow song, which normally meant Matt wasn't too interested. But Andrea grabbed his hand and led him out onto the floor. "I don't know how to dance like this," Matt said apologetically.

"Don't worry," she smiled. "It's not hard."

Andrea placed Matt's left hand on her waist and took his right hand in her left. They were still a few inches apart, but it was the closest Matt had ever been to a girl, not counting his mother. Her hand felt warm in his, and he hoped his fingers weren't too sweaty. He and Andrea moved around in a circle, looking at the other dancers and not saying anything to each other.

When the song was over, Andrea stepped back and said, "Thanks."

Matt nodded and said, "Yeah." What a stupid thing to say, he thought. Why hadn't he said thanks too?

Principal Walker and the parents were already turning up the lights and volunteers were beginning to pick up the soda cans.

Phil came up to Matt, Andrea and Marcia at the edge of the dance floor, but Matt realized that he hadn't seen Jake and his cousins since they had gone outside.

"Marcia, do you know where Jake and those guys went?" Matt asked.

Marcia looked at Andrea and then back at Matt. "You better ask him yourself," she said. She didn't look happy.

Andrea grabbed Matt's right arm gently. "I have to go now," she said. "My mom said she'd pick Marcia and me up outside at 10:30 and it's past that now.

Thanks. I had a really good time tonight. I'll see you in school Monday."

"I had fun too," Matt replied. He felt like he should say more but what exactly? He waved to Andrea and Marcia as they headed toward the gym door.

"Mattster!" It was Jake. He had been in the back corner of the gym with Cody and Vance and some older kids. "Where are the girls?"

"They left," Matt said. "Where'd you guys go, anyway?"

Vance, a strange smirk on his face, piped up. "We just went for a hike."

"Yeah," said Cody. "A nice long hike."

What were these guys talking about? Matt thought. He was just about to ask when Jake said, "Sorry guys, we've gotta go. My mom and dad are picking us up outside, like ten minutes ago."

Matt and Phil said goodbye to Jake and his cousins and watched them walk away. Then they headed to the coat check to pick up their jackets. "You guys are the last ones here," said the ninth-grade girl working the counter. "But I've got this one left too. Do you guys know who it belongs to?"

Matt recognized the red coat with the black lining immediately. It was Jake's. "That's my friend's," he said. "I'll get it to him."

Matt and Phil walked up Anderson Crescent together in the cool of the spring evening. It was nice to get some fresh air after being in that sweaty gym all night, and the nighttime hush was a relief to their ears. "What did you think of the dance?" Matt asked.

"It was good," Phil said. "That DJ had some killer speakers. My dad sells those downtown, they're like $3,000 a pair."

They were already at Anderson and Seventh. Phil only had a few blocks left to walk to his grandmother's store. "I'll catch you later," Matt said, smiling at his buddy. "See you Monday for sure."

The lights were on in the living room and Matt's mom was on the sofa with a cup of tea, reading the *Post*. She looked up as he came in. "How's my dancin' machine?" she asked.

"It was pretty fun," Matt said. "I'm not much of a machine, though."

Matt told his mother all about the dance, leaving out the part about hanging out with Andrea for the night and especially the part about slow dancing with her at the very end.

"I'm tired, though," he said. "And I've got hitting practice again in the morning with Charlie."

Matt was still carrying Jake's red jacket when he reached his room. He shoved it into his baseball equipment bag. That way he would be sure to remember to return it to Jake at Monday's game. Matt undressed, carefully hung up his clothes and jumped into bed. He was really tired, but something was bothering him. Just what had Jake and his cousins meant at the dance about taking a long hike? He knew he was on the outside of an inside joke but he couldn't figure it out.

Just as he was about to nod off, it hit him. "A long hike." Those were exactly the words Vance had used at Long Lake a couple of weeks ago. Jake and his cousins must have gone outside to smoke a joint. At the school dance! It all made sense now. That was why Marcia had come back so soon. Her dad was a drug and alcohol counselor for the school district, and she definitely wouldn't have been comfortable with that. And it also explained why Jake and his cousins had spent the rest of the dance by themselves.

What was Jake doing? Matt once again felt distant from his longtime friend. But he was kind of glad he hadn't clued into what was happening with Jake and his cousins earlier that night. At least they hadn't pressured him into going outside.

As he drifted off to sleep, Matt couldn't help but worry about his friend.

chapter ten

As soon as he finished breakfast the next morning, Matt grabbed his baseball glove, cap and batting helmet and jumped on his bike for the ride to South Side Middle School. By the time he arrived at the school, Charlie had already hauled out the pitching machine and had it set up on the mound.

"Sorry," Matt said as he parked his bike. "Am I late?"

Charlie shook his head. "I just wanted to mess around with this machine a bit to make sure I had it working before you got here," he said.

After a few warm-up swings, Charlie called for Matt to get into the batter's box. "I thought you did pretty well against Forshaw the other day," he told Matt. "Let's get to work."

Matt stood in the box as Charlie again fed balls into the whirring pitching machine. They were coming across the plate regularly now, about letter high and fast. But after missing the first few pitches, Matt began to connect consistently with the yellow practice balls, spraying them around the infield and nearly hitting Charlie a few times.

"We're at seventy now," the manager said. "Not many guys in the league are faster than this. I'll put it up to seventy-five. That's about as quick as you're ever going to see it."

The pitches were coming slightly faster now, but still across the plate. Within a few minutes, Matt was smacking three out of four at the higher speed.

Matt ran around the diamond collecting all of the balls he had hit and bringing them back to Charlie. As Matt gathered the balls, Charlie was tinkering with the pitching machine. "Okay, Matt," he said. "We'll try one more bag, but I'm mixing it up this time."

Matt returned to the batter's box. He wondered what, exactly, Charlie meant by "mixing it up."

The first pitch was another chest-high fastball. Matt swung confidently, poking it into right field. That was a serious hit because these softer practice balls didn't travel nearly as far as a real baseball.

Charlie dropped the next ball into the machine. It was high and inside. Matt had to duck to get out of the way. "What are you doing, Charlie?" he yelled. "Trying to go for my head?"

Charlie grinned and chuckled from behind the

machine. "You want to learn how to stand in there, don't you?" he said. "This is how you do it. By doing it."

Matt realized Charlie was right. How did this kid, who couldn't even run, know so much about baseball? He settled back into the box and took a practice cut. The next pitch was outside. He left that one alone. The next was down the middle, and he swung and missed. The following two were inside, forcing him to duck out of the way.

By the time they had gone through the fifty practice balls, Matt was tired from swinging and ducking and bobbing. But Charlie had a satisfied look on his face. "You just did fifty pitches at seventy-five miles an hour," he said. "Nobody in this league is going to throw faster, or wilder, than I just had this machine throwing. If you do what you did today in the next game, you'll be in the starting lineup before you know it."

Matt knew Charlie was right. During this practice session, he had convinced himself that if a ball was speeding toward him, he could get out of the way in time. Otherwise, he could stand in there and take a cut. He was surging with confidence.

Matt jogged out to the field and began picking up the balls again. Charlie was folding up the pitching machine and preparing to take it back inside. "Hold up," Matt said. "Let me help you with that."

They grunted and groaned as they moved the clunky apparatus back into the locker room. Matt was amazed at how much weight Charlie could handle even with his bum leg. "Hey, Charlie," he blurted out. "What's wrong with your leg, anyway?"

Charlie didn't look the least bit embarrassed or self-conscious. "About a year ago, I started getting a sore knee and then my hip starting hurting," he said matter-of-factly. "My parents took me to a couple of doctors, and they did some x-rays and other tests and they finally told me I have Perthes' disease."

Matt screwed up his face. "What's that?"

"Well, basically not enough blood was getting to my hip and the top of my thigh bone got all soft. It's supposed to get better on its own, but for the next year or two, I'm in this thing to keep stuff in the right place," Charlie said, pointing to his large brace. "It sorta sucks for sports, though."

"Does it hurt?" Matt asked.

"Not really," Charlie said. "If I'm on it too much, like on my skateboard, it can get sore at night."

Matt didn't know Charlie could skateboard. In fact, he didn't know much about the eighth-grade manager beyond all the things he did for the South Side team.

"How do you know so much about baseball?" Matt asked. "Like how to teach hitting and stuff like that?"

"I read a lot of books. *The Science of Hitting, Baseball Basics*...that sort of thing," Charlie said. "Plus I watch Coach all the time, pick up things he does. That's kind of what I want to do...be a coach. If I can, that is."

Matt nodded. He had to admire Charlie for his attitude. It wouldn't be easy wearing that brace while everybody else his age was running around free.

"I've got to go," Charlie said. "Nice work out there. Just remember what we did today when you're up next game."

"Thanks, Charlie," Matt said. "I appreciate you doing this."

Matt rode home, extremely happy with the practice session and carrying a newfound admiration for Charlie. Just because a kid couldn't run didn't mean he couldn't be a valuable member of a team.

chapter eleven

It promised to be the toughest test of the season so far for the South Side Stingers. The Churchill Bulldogs had won their first two games of the schedule, just like South Side, and the two teams were meeting in a Monday match-up on the Stingers' field.

Matt could tell all his teammates were excited about the game. On the way to school that morning, he and Jake and Phil had talked about only one topic—baseball. Friday's dance and what had happened with Jake and his cousins had faded well into the background.

"Churchill is tough," Phil said. "Especially Sid Logan. Remember that kid from Little League? He was major-league fast even then."

Matt did remember. Sid Logan was a year older than he was but looked like he was about twenty-five. Logan had huge shoulders and long arms and threw with a sidearm delivery that made it difficult to spot the ball as it was coming toward the plate.

None of them—not even Jake—had been able to hit Logan in Little League. In fact, his team had gone all the way to the Little League World Series regionals in his final year. Now the Churchill star was in his second middle school season and people were already starting to whisper that he could be a big-league prospect down the road.

"We'll get to Logan today," Jake proclaimed proudly. "We're all better than we were back in Little League. And he's just one guy."

Matt nodded. But he was thinking that one guy was going to be awfully tough to hit.

Matt almost knocked Andrea over as he hurried into the classroom for advisory period. The collision knocked a book out of her hand. As he bent over to pick it up, they gently knocked heads. "Good thing we danced better than this," she said.

Matt smiled. He had worried it might be a little weird between the two of them after slow dancing on Friday night, but things were just like they always had been. She was pretty cool, not all uptight like other girls. He liked that about her.

Amar leaned ahead in his desk as Matt sat down. "You guys an item now?" he asked.

Matt felt flustered. "No," he said. "I mean, I don't know."

Amar chuckled quietly as he sat back in his desk. Matt found himself a little annoyed. What was Amar giving him grief about? What was he supposed to do? Not talk to Andrea?

The school day dragged on, just as most days did in June. School was nearly finished for the year and it seemed like everybody—from the students to the teachers and Principal Walker—were just hanging on now until the end.

The only thing that didn't feel like that was baseball. A buzz was building in the school around the undefeated Stingers team. When the final buzzer went at 3:35, Matt ran to his locker, tossed his books inside, grabbed his baseball equipment bag and headed to the locker room. He pulled on his uniform pants and jersey and laced up his cleats just like always—the left before the right. It was a superstition he had believed in since his first tyke's soccer game. No use in breaking with tradition now.

The Stingers crisply ran through infield practice as the Bulldogs arrived and took the visitors' dugout. Out of the corner of his eye, Matt saw Sid Logan stretching on the field. With his wide, sloping shoulders, lantern-shaped jaw and his massive forearms, Logan looked like a grown man. He looked even bigger to Matt than he had in Little League.

As the Stingers headed to their dugout to let Churchill take infield practice, Matt noticed Officer Peters standing behind the fence by the dugout. Sitting attentively next to him was Joker, his black German shepherd. Matt waved and his neighbor waved back.

"Good luck," Officer Peters shouted.

Matt looked up in the stands. He knew his mom couldn't make it for this game, but he checked anyway, just in case. She wasn't in her usual seat, but the Piancatos were there and so, for the second straight game, was Phil's elderly grandmother. Too bad Mom couldn't be here, he thought. But there were plenty of other friendly faces in the crowd.

The Stingers were in the field first, and, as usual, Coach Stephens was starting Kevin Archibald at second. Also as usual, Matt held the stats clipboard. Oh well, he thought to himself. Somebody had to do it. Charlie couldn't do everything to keep this team running smoothly.

Besides being a match-up of undefeated teams, this was also going to be a battle of ace pitchers. While Churchill was throwing Sid Logan, the Stingers were countering with Steve White. There wouldn't be many hits to spare today.

White had only thrown a couple of pitches to the first Churchill batter when the commotion started. Matt could hear a dog going crazy, barking and yelping and straining at his leash. Matt realized it was Joker. It wasn't at all like Officer Peters' dog to be this undisciplined, but Joker was going absolutely nuts. He was trying desperately to get into the dugout, and he seemed to be intent at reaching the pile of Stingers' equipment bags lying in the corner.

Steve White stopped pitching and the plate umpire called time. Everybody on the diamond and those in the stands who had the right angle were watching as Joker pulled Officer Peters right into the dugout. The dog was now rooting amongst the equipment bags, dead set on getting to something. Joker suddenly settled on one bag, then sat there and looked up at Officer Peters, as if he was waiting for something.

"Joker!" Officer Peters was yelling a command at his dog in a booming voice that Matt had never heard before. "Heel!"

As the dog moved away, Matt realized that Joker had been sitting on his equipment bag. What was the dog so interested in, he wondered? He noticed Officer Peters bending over to examine the bag. Then in a few seconds his neighbor was gone. "Come on," Officer Peters chided the riled shepherd. "I'm taking you home now. You've already created enough racket here."

Parents and students in the stands laughed and the players smiled as Officer Peters looked at the umpire and apologetically shrugged his shoulders. Now that the distraction was over, the game could resume.

And what a game it turned out to be. As expected, Logan and White dueled each other all the way to the end, with neither giving up a run in the first six innings. In fact, Logan had surrendered just a single hit, a sharp double to Jake in the fourth inning, and he had walked just three batters. White had been slightly more human, allowing a pair of hits. But he had six strikeouts, one for each inning worked.

Once again, Coach Stephens had used Matt as a replacement at second base for Kevin Archibald, who moved into the outfield in the top of the fifth inning. Matt hadn't been up to bat yet, though, nor had anything been hit his way in the infield.

Sid Logan was up first for the Bulldogs in the seventh and final inning. Although he was a star pitcher, the towering eighth-grader was clumsy with the bat. White had him whiffed on three straight pitches as the dark-haired, swarthy Logan swung from the heels on each one. Matt couldn't help but think Logan would belt it into another time zone if he ever managed to connect.

White got the next Churchill batter to fly out to Jake at shortstop. That left just one Bulldog hitter, catcher Jimmy Flynn, whom Matt remembered as the point guard from the Churchill basketball team. Steve White was still throwing hard, but Flynn managed to slice a fastball, chopping the ball hard toward second base. Matt had to move quickly to his right, but he stabbed his glove skyward and grabbed the ball as it ricocheted off the clay infield. He wheeled and threw to Dave Tanner for the out, retiring the side.

White trotted over to give Matt a high five, clearly happy at the defensive play that helped preserve seven straight scoreless innings.

The South Side pitcher was obviously proud of himself as he sauntered off the field to cheers from the home crowd. He even doffed his cap to the stands, which seemed to Matt to be a bit much. Regardless, it felt good to help out a teammate, even if White wasn't his favorite teammate.

Tempering that feeling, though, was the Stingers' batting order. Matt knew he was up third—that meant there was no way to avoid facing the fireballing Sid Logan. The butterflies were already building up in his stomach.

Dave Tanner was first up, and although he was usually a pretty reliable hitter, the big first baseman went down swinging on four pitches. Next came Howard Berger, who grounded out weakly to short. Matt already had his batting helmet in hand, and Charlie was handing him his favorite bat. It was too late to back out now.

"Remember what we worked on," Charlie said quietly, out of earshot of the rest of the Stingers. "Just think of Logan as a gigantic pitching machine. He's not throwing any harder than what I gave you on Saturday."

Matt strode to the plate. With two out, everything was riding on his shoulders. If he didn't keep the inning alive, they would have to go to an extra frame. Steve White's arm looked like it was tiring. This was South Side's best chance for the win. He had to help make it happen.

Matt eased into the batter's box, tapped his bat on the plate and cocked it up behind his shoulders. He could feel his arms shaking slightly. Was that nerves or fear? He didn't have time to think about it. In a blur, Logan released the ball. It whizzed just inches past his nose, high and inside. Ball one.

"Good eye, Matty!" It was Charlie, standing at the edge of the dugout. "Way to stand in there."

Matt suddenly realized that's exactly what he had done. Sid Logan, the biggest, meanest pitcher in the league had just delivered him some chin music and he hadn't ducked away. He suddenly felt a lot more confident.

The next pitch was just as fast and it nicked the outside corner of the plate. Matt let it go by. "Steee-rikke!" the ump called. It was 1 and 1. Logan aimed for the same spot on the third pitch but missed by a few inches. On the next pitch, he was inside once more. Matt was up 3 and 1 in the count.

Matt knew the Churchill pitcher would have to offer him something good this time. And sure enough, Logan delivered a blistering fastball across the middle, letter-high. Matt swung with all his might, but just missed the pitch, ticking it foul down the third base line.

It was full count. The fans in the stands and players in both dugouts were on the edge of their seats. Logan wound up and his arm shot forward. The ball was headed inside, but not enough to let go. Matt swung hard. Crack! The ball took off like a jackrabbit, bounding between first and second. He ran as hard as he could to first base and easily made it in time. It was a clean single. He had kept the inning alive.

Matt glanced at Charlie by the dugout. A huge smile broke out across the manager's face and his brown eyes lit up. Matt had never seen him look so happy. He saw Charlie turn to Coach Stephens in the dugout and high-five him.

Kevin Archibald was up next for South Side. He was a red-haired, freckle-faced ninth-grader who never said much but played steadily both in the field and at the plate. Nothing seemed to rattle "Archie" much, which is likely why he started at second base ahead of Matt.

Logan bore down against Archibald, grunting as

he delivered the first pitch. It was wild and to the outside, passing the Churchill catcher. Matt shot off first and made it to second standing up. He was in scoring position now.

Archibald managed to work Logan to a full count too. On the deciding pitch, the big Churchill chucker put a fastball across the plate right at the Stinger hitter's knees. Archibald responded, stroking the ball into right field. Matt was off like a shot with the hit, eyes on third base where base coach Pete Winters was waving him on. He rounded the bag on the outside and headed full steam for home, just as the Bulldogs' right fielder pivoted and delivered the throw.

Matt and the baseball converged on home plate together. Six feet out, Matt went into the slide they had worked on in practice. As the ball sailed into Jimmy Flynn's glove, Matt was sliding underneath the Bulldog catcher's legs. "Safe!" yelled the umpire. The stands and the Stingers' dugout went nuts.

Matt was elated. He jumped off the ground and ran toward his teammates, getting a high five from each of them. Coach Stephens met him at the dugout steps. "You showed me something today, Matt," he said. "I think Charlie's pretty happy too."

Matt looked at Charlie in the dugout. He was already gathering up the stray equipment. Matt ambled down the stairs to help him out. It was the least he could do for a kid who had helped him so much.

chapter twelve

After showering and changing into a pair of shorts and flip-flops, Matt headed home. The feeling in the Stingers' locker room had been worth savoring, but he wanted to get back to his house as quickly as possible and share the news with his mom—about South Side's big win and about his big breakthrough at the plate.

By the time he was a half-block from home, Matt could see her green Toyota Camry was already in the driveway. But there was another vehicle in front of his house too. It was a white and blue city police cruiser. Matt's heart leapt into his throat. What was going on? Was Mom okay? Was it Mark? He sprinted to the house and up the front steps.

Throwing open the screen door, Matt called out, "Mom? Is everything okay?"

"We're in here, Matt." The voice came from the living room. But it wasn't his mother's. It belonged to Neil Peters. A wave of relief ran through his body. So that's why the police car was here.

"Hey, Mom," he said, entering the room. "You should have seen our game..." Matt stopped in mid-sentence. He could tell something was wrong. Both his mother and Officer Peters looked serious. Neither one was smiling.

"Matt, come over here and sit down," Mom said firmly, patting the sofa beside her.

This couldn't be good news, he thought. And he was right.

"Matt, you probably noticed Joker going crazy at your game today, right?" Officer Peters said, looking him directly in the eyes. "Do you know why he did that?"

Matt shook his head. He wasn't sure what Officer Peters was getting at.

"Joker is specially trained as a drug dog," the officer continued. "He only reacts like that when he's sniffed out something, like marijuana or cocaine. When he stops and points at something or barks like crazy, like he did today, that means he's found drugs."

Matt didn't understand what Officer Peters was saying. Why was he talking about drugs? There weren't any drugs in the South Side dugout.

"I checked, Matt, and Joker was pointing at your equipment bag," Officer Peters said. "Is there anything you want to tell us?"

Matt felt himself growing hot and confused. Tell them about what? He had absolutely no idea what his neighbor was talking about.

"No way," he cried out. "You don't think I had drugs in my bag, do you?" He stared at Mom, pleadingly.

There was a worried look in her brown eyes. "Matt, we're not going to be mad at you if you want to tell us the truth," she said softly.

"But there's nothing to tell," he insisted. "Joker must have been wrong. Mom, I don't know anything about any drugs. I sure didn't have any in my equipment bag."

Matt still had the long black bag draped over his right shoulder. "Look," he said. "There's nothing but baseball gear in here."

He dumped the bag on the living room floor. His brown leather mitt, black cleats, dirty socks, Stingers uniform and batting glove spilled out. Tears were welling up in Matt's brown eyes. He tried to stifle them, but he couldn't.

"I was just out watching your game today, Matt," Officer Peters said. "So technically, Joker and I were off-duty. I've talked to your mother and I'm not going to do anything with this. But I'm always around if you want to talk. You know that, right?"

Matt nodded silently. But he couldn't help feeling angry with Officer Peters for suspecting him. He was even mad at Joker. What a stupid dog. This was brutal. Both his mom and his neighbor were taking the word of a German Shepherd over him.

Officer Peters walked to the front door. "Gail, I'm around if you need help," he said to Matt's mom. "And, Matt, remember that goes for you too. Especially for you."

The officer cast a long look at Matt, as if searching for some sort of clue within his eyes. Then he waved and walked out the door.

Matt approached his mother, palms outstretched. "Mom, I swear, I've got no idea what this is all about," he said, desperate for her to believe him.

"Okay, Matt," she said. "We'll forget about this for now. But if you do want to talk about something, anything, you just ask, all right? I get worried about you growing up so fast."

With that, she reached out and grabbed her son, pulling him toward her. Even at twelve, going on thirteen, her hugs still felt good. But once they had separated, Matt began to fixate on the mystery of Joker and the equipment bag.

He went upstairs to his room and flopped onto his bed. He pulled out his iPod Shuffle, flipped in the ear buds and put it on random. The Black-Eyed Peas blasted out from the tiny music machine. He always found that listening to loud music, alone, was the best way to think something through.

Matt was reeling. Now both his mom and his neighbor—not to mention Joker—suspected he had something to do with drugs. But he had never so much as even tried marijuana. Matt knew many of the kids at South Side had, even some of the seventh-graders. Even Jake had tried it. Mom might be surprised to hear about that.

Then it hit him. Jake! Jake's red jacket had been in his baseball bag at the start of the game this afternoon. He must have left something in his pocket from the night of the dance. That's why Joker had gone nuts sniffing out Matt's bag. Matt had returned the jacket to Jake, but not until after the game in the locker room. That explained everything. Everything, that is, except what to do now.

Matt could easily clear himself, make Mom and Officer Peters stop worrying about him, if he just told them about the jacket and Jake smoking pot with his cousins. But that would also get Jake into a ton of trouble with his parents, not to mention Coach Stephens. Still, if Matt didn't tell his mom, she was probably going to think it was him, maybe even think that she couldn't trust him anymore. That was no good, either. This was completely unfair. Jake had made the wrong choices here but Matt was the one paying the price.

That night, as he tried to go to sleep, Matt wrestled with what he should do. There was no easy answer. Somewhere in the strange space between consciousness and sleep, a gigantic, pointy-eared Joker was following him around his house, sniffing him and growling every time he moved.

chapter thirteen

Matt got up early Tuesday morning, hustling to get dressed, eat his breakfast and get out the door. He was leaving home a good fifteen minutes before normal today and he was riding his bike. It wasn't like he wanted to get to school early or anything. It was just that he didn't want to run into Jake. Not today.

He and Jake had been friends since pre-school, but this morning Matt didn't want to have anything to do with him. He was mad at his buddy and he wasn't sure what he would say if they did meet. So he pedaled hard up Anderson Crescent, past the oak tree at which he usually met Phil and Jake and right on to school. Those guys would just have to walk in without him today.

As Matt was locking up his bike in the rack, he heard a familiar sound. Crack! Then a few seconds of silence. Crack! He knew what it was right away. It was barely 8:00 AM, but somebody was already taking batting practice.

Curious, Matt walked over to the diamond. Might as well, he thought. He was so early for school he had nothing better to do. There was Andrea, wearing her full South Side Stingers softball uniform—white and maroon with shorts and high socks—and standing at the plate. And on the mound, working behind the pitching machine was none other than Charlie.

"Five more," Charlie yelled. Andrea nodded her head. Five blazing fast pitches followed. Andrea put four of them into the outfield with a sharp confident swing of her bat.

"Thanks, Charlie," Andrea smiled. "I owe you some cookies."

"Chocolate chip," Charlie grinned back. "No, make that double chocolate chip."

Matt gave Charlie a hand rolling the pitching machine back into the storage room while Andrea collected the practice balls and her gear. Afterward, the three sat in the bleachers. It was a beautiful spring day, with the sun already giving off just enough heat to make it short-sleeve comfortable.

"When are you going to be able to play?" Matt asked Andrea.

She looked at Charlie. "I think this afternoon," she said. "We've been getting in some extra hitting for the last couple of weeks. Charlie's got me ready."

"Yeah, he's helped me out too," Matt said, playfully pulling the Yankees cap Charlie was wearing down over his eyes. "And I didn't even have to bake him anything."

Charlie laughed. "Hill, I wouldn't trust you to make toast."

Charlie suddenly looked at his watch and rose quickly. "I've got to get going," he said. "I've got a math test first thing this morning. Hargraves always gives brutal tests."

Matt and Andrea waved to Charlie as he walked away, struggling to work up a fast pace because of the brace on his leg. Matt could tell Charlie was in a good mood. He liked it when his work was appreciated. Then again, who didn't?

"So, you're playing today. That's great," Matt said, turning to Andrea, who looked so much different in a softball uniform, with her long blond hair in a ponytail pulled through the back of her purple Stingers cap.

It was the first time he had talked to Andrea alone since the dance. He had wondered if things might be a little awkward between them, but they weren't.

"Are you coming?" she asked.

"Sure, yeah," Matt said. "Gotta show the old school spirit, right?"

Andrea smiled. But it didn't last long. A look of concern came over her face, like she was remembering something negative.

"I'm glad you're here early this morning," she said. "I wanted to talk to you about something, but not around your friends.

"It's about the dance. Remember when Jake and those guys and Marcia went outside? I couldn't tell you about it then, but Marcia said Jake and his cousins were smoking a joint."

Matt didn't say anything.

"Whatever those guys do is up to them," Andrea continued. "But it wasn't cool with Marcia. I don't think she'll be hanging out with Jake anymore. He sort of ditched her too."

Matt understood. He felt like he should defend Jake. But he also felt like Marcia was right. Jake had just taken off on her after arranging the whole dance thing with the four of them. And with Marcia's dad being a drug and alcohol counselor, he was sure she would have felt pretty weird about seeing them smoke a joint.

"I sort of figured out what happened," Matt said solemnly. "And Marcia's not the only one who's pissed about it."

Matt wasn't sure why, but he felt he could tell Andrea about the dilemma he was facing with Jake. He told her about the night at Long Lake and about the drugs in Jake's jacket and about the mess he was now in with his mom and Officer Peters.

"I don't know what to do about it," he said, hoping she might have an idea.

"I think you have to talk to Jake," Andrea said. "You guys have been friends for a long time. He probably doesn't even know about the trouble he's caused for you."

The warning bell rang. That meant just five minutes before the first class of the morning. "I've got to go," he said. "Good luck in your game."

Matt had trouble concentrating all day. Mostly he was thinking about Jake and how he should approach his friend. But he was also thinking about Andrea. Nothing in particular, just thinking about her.

When the final buzzer rang at 3:35, Matt dumped his books, grabbed his backpack and pedaled to the ball diamond. The South Side girls were just taking the field for infield practice. Andrea was playing shortstop. She was fielding grounders with a huge smile on her face.

Matt didn't see Jake walking up behind him. But he felt the arms wrap around his head and twist his neck. "Full-on WWE submission hold," Jake yelled. "Give up, dude. I've got you in the stultifying sleeper of death hold."

Normally Matt would have joined right in with the clowning around. But he didn't feel like joking with Jake right now. Jake could read his serious look and toned down the wrestling shtick. "I need to talk to you about something," Matt said.

"What's up, Mattster?" Jake said.

In a few seconds, Matt had told his friend everything—about the jacket in the equipment bag, Joker, Officer Peters and his mom. Jake looked stunned, taking it all in slowly.

"That sucks," he said, shaking his head side to side. "What are you going to do?"

"I don't know," Matt said, leaving Jake an opening to make a suggestion of his own.

Just then a car horn honked. Matt looked in the direction of the sound and saw the Piancatos' long red station wagon in the parking lot. "I've gotta boogey," he said. "I'll talk to you about this later, okay? Just chill, man."

Just chill? That was the best Jake could do? Matt was furious. Jake was easy-going, sure, but this was ridiculous. Matt was in huge trouble because of Jake and all he could say was "That sucks" and "Just chill."

Normally on such a perfect spring afternoon, watching a softball game in the stands, Matt would have been in a terrific mood. But he couldn't shake the worry over his situation. What was he going to do to make things right with his mom and without alienating Jake?

The South Side girls had a powerful team this season, and getting Andrea back in the lineup made the Stingers that much better. Churchill was no match for them. In her first game since returning from her injury, Andrea went two-for-four with a double and the Stingers won 10-0.

Matt was happy for Andrea as he walked home from South Side. But the situation with his mom and Jake was still troubling him. By the time he reached the front door, he could smell Mom's chili cooking. That made him feel a bit better. He loved chili, and Mom always made garlic toast to go with it.

"Hey, Matt," she called out as he came in the door. "Wash up. I've got supper ready. I've got to show a house to clients tonight so we're eating early."

Matt joined his mom at the table for dinner. The chili was awesome. The two chatted about their days and Matt was just about to help himself to a second bowl when his mom cleared her throat.

"Matt, I talked to Mr. Evans today," she said. "He's running a weekly group educational session for kids. It's every Sunday for two months and it's only for two hours. I'd like you to start going."

Mr. Evans was Marcia's dad and the school district's drug and alcohol counselor.

"What for?" he said. "I don't need to go to that. I told you, I've got nothing to do with drugs."

"I know what you told me and I believe you," Mom said. "But just the same, I want you to take this session. It won't hurt, right? And there will probably be some kids there that you know."

Matt doubted that. He was angry. It felt like his mom didn't believe him, didn't trust him. "No way," he said. "I'm not going."

"Then you're not playing baseball either."

Matt couldn't believe the words had come out of his mother's mouth. She was going to use baseball to make him do this. This was definitely unfair. He was furious.

"Why are you doing this?" he asked, getting up from the table abruptly. "I'm outta here."

"Come back and finish your..." Mom didn't even get to finish her sentence. Matt was already in his room.

An hour later, there was a knock on the bedroom door. "I'm going to show that house now," Mom said. "Make sure you do your homework."

Matt grunted. "Okay. Bye." He still didn't want to talk to her.

By 9:00 PM, she wasn't home yet, and Matt figured she was probably writing up an offer for clients. He decided to head to bed. He was tired, partly from getting up early and partly from the fight with his mother. Lying in bed, looking up at the patterns in the ceiling plaster, Matt couldn't figure a way out of this one. He would certainly have to go to the group counseling sessions. At least that would probably fix things with him and Mom. As for Jake, Matt wasn't sure what to do.

chapter fourteen

Matt sat at the front of the classroom, doodling on a piece of scrap paper. He was writing *Stingers–5 wins, 0 losses* and drawing a picture of a trophy beside the team name, oblivious to what Mr. Evans was saying at the front of the room.

"How about you, Matt?" Suddenly the eyes of fifteen other kids were fixed upon him.

Matt didn't have a clue what Mr. Evans had asked him. "I'm sorry," he mumbled sheepishly. "I guess I missed the question."

Mr. Evans was a tall, stocky man with long gray-white hair that almost touched his broad shoulders. He was dressed casually, in a pair of jeans and a T-shirt. He looked like he played basketball at one time, Matt thought.

"I was just asking everybody here whether they had ever done something that later they regretted, and then didn't know how to make things right," Mr. Evans said. "How about you? Have you ever done something like that?"

"Sure, I guess," Matt said. He could think of plenty of things. But the thing that came to mind first was what Jake had done. And now he was paying the price for it. On a beautiful sunny spring day, instead of playing hoops with Phil and Amar and Jake at Anderson Park, he was cooped up inside this stuffy classroom.

"What we're trying to get through to you in this session is that everybody makes mistakes and that it's okay to make them," Mr. Evans said. "The most important thing is how you learn from them. Do you keep making the same mistakes until they lead to one that changes your life in a negative way? Or do you pick up enough smarts along the way that those mistakes add up to valuable experience rather than trouble?"

What Mr. Evans was saying made sense to Matt. He had made mistakes during his first year of middle school—they had almost got him thrown off the basketball team—but he had learned from them. Or at least he thought he had.

"We know kids are going to experiment," Mr. Evans said, speaking to everybody in the room. "I did when I was a kid."

That produced a few chuckles from the students

in the classroom. None of them could picture Mr. Evans as a kid.

"Sometimes drugs and alcohol are part of that experimenting," Mr. Evans continued. "And what we're trying to do here is arm you with enough information so that you can make good choices.

"This is an open class, but nothing said here goes beyond the door. I'm not here to judge you or to tell your parents or teachers or the police what you're up to. I'm here to help you—to provide you with information or advice or assistance if you need it."

A hand went up in the back of the room. A skinny girl with spiky black hair and a silver tank top had a question.

"Does that mean you're not going to narc on us if we tell you something?" she said.

More laughs. "No." Mr. Evans grinned. "I'm not the narcing type."

Despite the fact he didn't want to be there, Matt couldn't help but take a liking to Mr. Evans. He was funny and seemed pretty cool for somebody who was old. Maybe this wouldn't be as bad as he thought.

The rest of the afternoon session was devoted to learning about different types of drugs and alcohol and the dangers of doing something stupid if you were high or drunk. At the very end of the class, Mr. Evans pulled out a clear baggie, with a line of green stuff at the bottom that looked like the spices Mom kept in the kitchen.

"Most of you may know this already, but this is what marijuana looks like," he said, holding up the bag.

"I know many of you think it's harmless, and some adults would probably agree. But there are things you should be aware of.

"For starters, nobody knows what's really in this bag. Whoever gives or sells it to you may not know what's in it. He or she likely got it from somebody else, who could have got it from somebody else. It could be marijuana. It could be parsley. It could be poison. The point is, you don't know."

Mr. Evans sat on the edge of his desk and leaned forward.

"I have to tell you, there is a real risk here, even with marijuana," he said. "The police tell me that these days, marijuana sometimes has something called crystal meth mixed into it. People are getting messed up and, without realizing it, are getting addicted to a drug that is far more dangerous. And when I said that nobody knows what is in marijuana, that goes double or triple for crystal meth. Crystal meth is a drug that people are mixing in their basements using battery chemicals, paint thinner and household cleaners. It is bad news. Believe me, you don't want any part of it.

"That's why more than ever—certainly more than when myself or your parents were in school—it is important to make good decisions. And if you make a bad one, it's important to realize it quickly and learn from it."

That was it. The session was over but Matt's brain was turning this information over and over. He had heard of crystal meth before but only in news stories on television. It was pretty scary to think that some of that junk could end up in a joint, maybe even a joint like Jake had smoked with his cousins.

Attending the counseling session had certainly put a crimp in Matt's Sunday schedule. Not only had he missed hoops, he was now severely squeezed for time to complete his social studies project. It was a pretty cool assignment—the students had been required to pick a country they knew nothing about and then develop a travel brochure for it. Matt had chosen Bolivia, a small South American country that he had learned produced much of the world's cocoa beans, which were the essential ingredient in chocolate. His slogan was *Bolivia, Your Chocolate Source.* It had a nice ring to it.

Matt was printing off pictures of Bolivia from the Internet to use in his brochure when the phone rang. He heard Mom answer it. "Matt, it's for you."

He bounded down the stairs and grabbed the cordless phone. "It's Jake," Mom said. "I forgot to tell you he called earlier this afternoon too."

"Hey, Jake," Matt said. Although things hadn't been the same between them, his anger had dissipated.

"Where were you today?" Jake asked. "I called about hoops. We had some killer threes at Anderson."

"I couldn't make it," Matt said solemnly. "I had something else going. I'm not going to be out on Sundays for about two months."

"You gone religious on me, son?" Jake joked. Matt didn't think it was funny. He took the phone upstairs and closed the door to his room.

"Actually, I'm tied up on Sundays because of you," he said, leaving the statement to hang in the air.

"What do you mean?" Jake asked. There was another long awkward pause.

Matt had been waiting for an opening, and here it was. He jumped at the chance. "My mom's making me go to a drug and alcohol counseling program that Marcia's dad runs. It's because of Joker sniffing your jacket in my bag and freaking out in the dugout."

Again, silence on the other end.

"Matt, I'm sorry, man. I feel bad. I didn't mean..."

"I know you didn't mean it, but it happened," Matt said. "Now I've gotta go to this thing for the next two months."

"Sorry, bud," Jake apologized again.

"Yeah, I know," Matt replied. "I just thought you should know, that's all. I've gotta go now. I've got this travel project to do for school."

Jake hung up. Matt knew he felt bad about what had happened, but part of him was pleased with that. Until now, Matt had been taking the full brunt of Jake's actions. It was only fair Jake shared in some of the discomfort.

Matt kept working on the project, cutting out pictures of Bolivian jungles and cocoa beans. A country full of chocolate. Not a bad place for a holiday at all.

chapter fifteen

Monday was a big day for Matt. Not only was his social studies project due, but the South Side Stingers had an important game that afternoon against the Middleton Marauders.

Middleton was on the north side of the city, so the South Side players had to put on their uniforms, hats and cleats right after school was out and quickly board a bus for the twenty-five-minute drive through city traffic. The Stingers carried a 5-0 record into this game and, with only three games left in the regular season, were looking like they would finish in first place in the league. Getting that top spot was crucial too, since only the best team in the regular season advanced to district playoffs. For the rest, baseball was over.

The Marauders were a strong team themselves. They were 4-1, with their only loss so far to the

Churchill Bulldogs. This road game was critical for the Stingers.

Middleton was an aging neighborhood that at one time had been the heart of the city. But as the region's population grew and the more affluent families settled in North Vale or South Side, Middleton had become neglected, a place where young families avoided moving, as long as they could afford to live somewhere else. As the bus neared the Middleton campus, Matt noticed that many of the buildings appeared run-down or even deserted. The same went for the school, a two-story red-brick building surrounded by pavement and partially covered with graffiti, some of which looked like the gang signs Matt had seen in movies.

Middleton's ball diamond wasn't much better. It was nothing like the facility at South Side, with its pristine white fences, electronic scoreboard and green grass. The Middleton field, in contrast, was surrounded by a chain-link fence that had holes in several places. The grass was scrubby, half-brown and dotted with weeds, and it looked like the scoreboard lights had long ago been rendered useless by vandalism.

It was quiet on the bus. Coach Stephens seemed to read what was going through his players' minds. "Don't let their diamond fool you guys," he warned. "These kids are ball players."

It was obvious from watching the Marauders' infield warm-up that Coach was right. Middleton had a handful of tiny, quick fielders who could cover an amazing amount of ground and were capable of making acrobatic catches. They also had a terrific junk-ball pitcher in David Martinez, another small-ish kid who wore a glove that seemed about two times too big for him.

Matt, Jake and Phil all knew Martinez well from Little League. Whenever their squad from Anderson Park made it a couple of rounds into a tournament, they had faced Martinez. The lefthander wasn't fast, but he was nearly impossible to hit. For a kid his age, he had an unusually effective assortment of off-speed pitches—a wicked curve and a change-up—that left batters swinging at air more often than not.

South Side was starting its own ace in lanky lefty Steve White, who seemed to be pitching better every game out. You could tell by the crisp tone of warm-ups that both teams were serious and looking forward to this one.

The Stingers and Marauders battled evenly for six innings, each scoring once and leaving a handful of runners stranded. Nobody in the Stingers' lineup was hitting Martinez, yet, but the Middleton pitcher had been a little wilder than usual, walking five batters. Meanwhile, White was shakier than Matt had ever remembered him being. He had only surrendered a single run, but he had been in trouble almost every inning and only some terrific plays by the South Side infield had bailed him out.

Matt had been glued to the South Side bench, clipboard and pencil in hand—his usual spot this season, it seemed. If a guy had to take statistics, though, at least this had been an exciting game to watch.

Just as South Side came up to bat in the top of the seventh, Coach Stephens cleared his throat and announced he was making a lineup change. "Hill, you're hitting for White," he said, looking at Matt. "You'll play second, Archibald you go to short, and Jake you pitch the last inning."

The move caught Matt off guard. White was up first in the batting order this inning. That meant Matt was suddenly going to the plate in one of the most important at-bats of the season for his team. He quickly pulled on his batting helmet, fumbling with the chin strap. Charlie grabbed Matt's favorite bat from his carefully arranged collection. "Like you can, Matt," Charlie said quietly, handing him the stick. "Like you can."

Matt strode to the plate. The hundred or so fans in the stands were chanting, "Strike him out! Strike him out!", as they had in support of Martinez for most of the game. But once he stepped into the batter's box and dug his cleats into the hard soil,

Matt tried to tune it all out and focus completely on the pitcher.

With the first pitch Matt felt as though everything was in slow motion. The ball appeared to be coming right over the plate at Little League speed. It looked fat and juicy enough to slug right over the...Matt's thoughts were rudely interrupted as his overly ambitious swipe at the baseball achieved nothing but air. "Steeerike!" the umpire bellowed, shooting out his right hand dramatically to signal the call.

Matt heard a few sniggers in the stands and in the Middleton dugout. He felt like a fool having taken such a big swing only to end up twisting around like a pretzel. But he was determined to keep his composure. All that extra batting practice had made him feel a lot more comfortable and confident in his ability at the plate.

Matt stepped out of the box to gather himself, as Coach Stephens always instructed his players to do. He knew Martinez wasn't throwing anything with speed. In fact, the Middleton ace hadn't thrown a fastball all game. It was either going to be the curve or the change-up, which is what the first pitch had been. And it was just a matter of Matt guessing right, and then executing.

Looking down the first-base line at Coach Stephens, Matt saw the coach tip his cap and then put his right hand in the back pocket of his uniform. This was the sign to "take" the next pitch, no matter where it was. Matt stepped into the box and waited, bat cocked. Martinez wheeled and threw. The ball seemed to be heading for the right-hand top corner of the plate as Matt watched intently, resisting the urge to swing. But as the pitch broke, it veered outside by about six inches. It was the curve ball all right, and it had missed the plate completely.

After stepping out again, Matt saw Coach fold his arms across his chest and then adjust his hat. He was telling Matt to swing away at the next pitch if it was good. As Martinez wound up, Matt had a strong feeling another change-up was coming his way. This time he patiently waited on the ball until he could gauge the speed. Lining it up calmly, he blooped the ball into left field for a single.

The South Side dugout erupted. Nobody had hit Martinez cleanly yet today. Not until Matt. Coach Stephens was pumped up too. "Nice at-bat, Hill," he said from his coaching box at first.

Archibald was up next. He went down swinging hard at the change-up magic of Martinez. But one wild pitch that got by the catcher during his at-bat allowed Matt to hustle down to second base. Howard Berger followed Archibald, but he grounded out quietly, moving Matt along to third.

There were two outs as Phil came to the plate. Matt knew that if anybody else on the South Side bench had figured out Martinez it would be Phil. Like most good catchers, he could quickly pick out a pitcher's tendencies, something that made him a dangerous hitter in the latter stages of any game.

Matt watched from third as Phil, a determined look on his broad face, worked Martinez to a two-and-two count. Then, just as Matt had done, he waited on the change-up, patiently stroking the ball into center field. Phil's hit scored Matt. South Side was ahead 2-1 with just a half-inning to go.

Those were all the hits Martinez would surrender, though. And as the Marauders trotted in from the field, they still seemed supremely confident in their ability to come back.

Jake hustled out of the dugout to the mound. He often relieved White or another starter in the late innings. Coach Stephens liked the fact Jake could throw hard and accurate for at least two innings. He was a great shortstop, but he was valuable to the Stingers as a late reliever as well.

Still, this had easily been Jake's worst game of the season. Matt had noticed that he didn't have the same confident bounce in his step today. He hadn't even managed a single hit off Martinez, walking once, grounding out and striking out on the Marauder pitcher's wicked curve ball.

The first Middleton batter was Martinez himself. He was a decent hitter, but no match for Jake's pure speed on this day. Four pitches later, Martinez was heading back to the dugout, shaking his head after a disappointing strikeout.

The Stingers were now two outs away from a huge win. With just Central and Mandela left on their schedule—both of which figured to be routine wins— a victory here could almost lock up first place.

Up next, however, was catcher Tommy Layne, a player that everybody on the South Side team knew well. Layne was a ninth-grade shortstop who had also probably been the city's best middle school basketball player for Middleton this past season. Hoops was Layne's first love, but his lean sinewy frame and huge hands were those of a pure athlete. The kid could hit and field too.

Jake caught Layne looking with the first pitch, a fastball. But when he tried to throw the same thing past Layne on the next offering, the Middleton senior wheeled on the pitch and drove a hard grounder straight at Matt, who was covering the hole between first and second.

Matt charged the grounder, thinking he had a good read on the ball. But at the last second it bounced high off a clump of grass at the edge of the unkempt Middleton infield and soared over his head. There was nothing he could do but watch it bounce into center field.

Layne seized the opportunity, hustling to second

before the South Side outfield could relay the ball in to Matt. The tying run was now aboard with just one out.

The next Middleton batter grounded weakly to Howard Berger at third. Layne held his position at second as Berger checked him off and then threw out the runner at first. It was two away. One more out would seal the win for the Stingers.

The Middleton crowd was on edge as Gustavo Martinez, the older brother of David, strode to the plate. "Gus! Gus! Gus!" the fans chanted as the muscular ninth-grader took his practice cuts. Martinez was the Marauders' best long-ball hitter. He had taken Steve White deep to center a couple of times today, but hadn't managed a hit.

Jake went into his windup and delivered a sizzling fastball that split the center of the plate. Martinez had been taking all the way, so he didn't even blink when the umpire signaled the first strike. On the next pitch, Jake got lucky. The ball slipped out of his grip as he delivered, floating out over the plate like a balloon. But it fooled Martinez, who had been expecting heat. He swung wildly, twisting himself up just as Matt had done on the first pitch from the younger Martinez.

Jake was nicely up on the count. Now he could afford to paint the corners, Matt thought. Jake wound up to deliver the third pitch. It was obvious from the grunt he emitted that he was trying to end this thing now. He put another fastball right down the middle, but this time Gus Martinez was ready.

The big dark-haired boy had timed it perfectly, bringing his bat around in a blur and transferring his weight to full effect. He caught the ball flush and sent a towering drive out to center field. Matt watched as it sailed far over his head. He already knew there would be no play on this one. Martinez had parked it over the fence and the ball bounced wildly off the asphalt of the school parking lot. Middleton had won the game 3-2. The Marauders' dugout erupted, dog-piling the elder Martinez as he crossed the plate.

Matt walked dejectedly off the field toward the dugout. He thought he felt about as bad as some-body could until he looked at Jake, who had hurled his glove down at the mound in disgust.

The Stingers quietly filed out of the dugout and back onto their bus. With that one hit, their hopes for the playoffs had been thrown into serious jeopardy. Jake slumped into a seat at the back of the bus. Matt slid into the double bench right in front of him.

"Tough one," Matt said quietly to his friend. "That kid can hit."

Jake was still looking at the floor of the bus. It was a few seconds before he spoke. "It was my fault," he said solemnly. "I shouldn't have given that kid anything to hit. I thought I had him after that second pitch. I got cocky."

Matt was just about to say something when Coach Stephens piped up from the front of the bus. "Listen up, guys," he said.

"We lost a tough one this afternoon. But we got beat by a great hit and a great hitter. Nobody should hang his head in this bus. You guys all played heads-up baseball. I couldn't ask for much better. Sometimes it's just not your day."

There was silence on the bus, but several players nodded their heads. Jake was still looking down at the floor.

"All right, let's shake it off," Coach continued. "Practice is Wednesday, just like always."

As the bus pulled into the South Side parking lot, Phil spied his parents' gold Lexus sedan idling. "I've gotta go," he said eagerly, grabbing his equipment and hustling to the front of the bus. "We're going out for dinner tonight. Grandma's eighty today."

Matt could see Phil's parents from the bus window and waved to them. Phil's grandmother spotted Matt and waved furiously. She had known him since he was in kindergarten and treated him like he was her own grandson. Whenever he and Phil hung out at her tiny corner grocery, she would pull out chips and candy and Cokes and spoil them rotten.

Phil's departure left Matt and Jake to walk home

together. Matt felt strangely awkward. They hadn't spoken much since their telephone conversation about the joint found in Matt's bag. For the first block down Anderson Crescent, neither said much.

"I couldn't concentrate out there today." Jake finally broke the ice. Matt thought that he had never seen his friend look so serious. His jaw was set and his blue eyes seemed weary.

"I've been thinking about what we talked about the other night," Jake continued. "You were right, Matt. What happened was totally unfair to you. I've kind of been acting like a jerk."

Matt couldn't argue there. But he felt he had to ease his buddy's worry. "I just wanted you to know what happened, Jake," he said. "It's not like I'm totally pissed at you or anything."

Jake cleared his throat. For a second, there was silence. Then he spoke. "You should be," he said. "You're in trouble because of something I did.

"I was thinking," he continued. "What about if I went with you to those Sunday things?"

"You mean with Mr. Evans?" Matt said. "Why would you want to do that?"

"It's not that I want to. It's just that I feel responsible. Why should you be stuck there by yourself?"

"But what will your parents say?" Matt asked. "They're bound to find out you're in Mr. Evans' group. They'll know something's up."

"They're going to know anyway," Jake said. "Because I'm going to tell them tonight."

"You sure you want to do that?" Matt said.

"Yeah, I'm sure," Jake said resignedly.

The Piancatos' station wagon pulled up beside them. Mr. Piancato rolled down the passenger window. "Hey, guys," he said. "How did you do?"

"We lost 3-2," Matt answered quickly. "But it was a pretty good game."

Jake looked at Matt as he opened the car door. "Later, man," he said.

"Good luck," Matt replied as he watched the car pull away. He was awfully glad not to be in Jake's shoes tonight.

chapter sixteen

There was definitely a buzz surrounding the ball team at school on Tuesday morning. But it didn't have anything to do with the boys' baseball squad. Instead, it was the Stinger girls who were basking in the limelight.

"Make sure you get out to the diamond this afternoon and catch the undefeated South Side Stingers against Middleton in girls' softball at its finest," Principal Walker said during the morning announcements.

"One more win this season and your Stingers are off to the regional playoffs. They deserve your support."

There was no mention of the boys' baseball team this morning. Yesterday's loss to Middleton had put a serious crimp in the team's playoff hopes. Even if they won the final two games, they would have to rely on both Middleton and Churchill losing one of their final two games. The chances of that happening were slim.

While disappointed with the way the season was playing out—both for him personally and for the team—Matt was happy for the girls and especially for Andrea, who was finding her groove as a shortstop and developing into one of the team's best players.

With no practice of his own to worry about that afternoon, Matt headed to the diamond with Phil to catch the girls' game. He hadn't seen Jake at school all day and neither had Phil. He didn't say anything to anybody else but Matt wondered whether Jake had gone ahead and broken the news about the joint to his parents the night before.

Phil and Matt cheered enthusiastically as the South Side girls cruised to an easy 8-1 win over Middleton, wrapping up first place and a spot in the playoffs. Andrea was enjoying her best game of the season so far, going two-for-three with a double and some terrific plays at shortstop. Matt knew wearing the cast all winter had meant she had been waiting a long time to go full-out in sports. It was good to see her so happy and doing so well.

After the game, Matt and Phil were walking down Anderson toward home when they heard a voice behind them. "Hey, guys, wait up!" It was Jake.

"Where were you, man?" Phil said as Jake puffed up. "We thought we'd see you at the girls' game for sure."

A sheepish look crossed Jake's hearty face. "Let's just say it was a long night out at Long Lake," he said ruefully, trying to make light out of what most certainly hadn't been a light situation.

Jake brought Phil and Matt up to speed. He had told his parents the previous night about smoking marijuana with his cousins. They had both been stunned. He had also told them about the jackpot Matt now found himself in, thanks to Jake.

"Sucks to be you," Phil said, half-jokingly. "Man, I had no idea about all this stuff. You guys hiding anything else from me?"

Jake looked directly at Matt. "I'm in so much trouble with my mom and dad," he said, shaking his head. "I'm like grounded for two weeks. I had to spend half the morning with them in the school counselor's office. And I'm done with baseball for this year."

The last sentence was the one that registered with Matt and Phil. Had he actually said "Done with baseball"?

"Mom and Dad totally freaked out," Jake continued. "They're super mad at Cody and Vance. They phoned their parents. And Matt, they phoned your mom too."

"What?" Matt said. "Why?"

"They said it was only fair to you. It was my jacket that Joker smelled, not your gear. They said it wasn't right that you were taking the blame for that...And they're right."

Matt suddenly felt elated and depressed all at the same time. It was a huge load off his shoulders that his mom would now know that he hadn't been involved with drugs. But at the same time, he felt bad for Jake and for the team. Without Jake in the lineup, South Side could probably kiss the playoffs goodbye.

"Guess you're off the hook for Sundays," Jake said to Matt. "My parents want me to take Mr. Evans' counseling sessions now."

They were already at the corner of Anderson and Seventh. "I know your parents are pissed," Matt said, looking at Jake. "But they'll get over it eventually."

"Hope so," Jake said glumly. And with that, he and Phil continued to walk toward Wong's Grocery where Jake, as usual, would catch the bus out to Long Lake.

Matt hesitated at the corner and watched as his two friends headed up Seventh. He knew Jake felt bad, but he also knew his friend had done the right thing. It was nice to have the old Jake back again.

Mom was in the kitchen, dicing up cucumber for a salad when she heard Matt come in the door. She stopped what she was doing and met him in the hallway. She had a smile on her face. "I got a call from Jake's mom and dad today," she said. "They explained to me what happened. I'm sorry I didn't have more faith in you, Matt."

"It's okay, Mom. I mean, what were you supposed to think, anyway? The dog freaked out on my equipment bag. It must have looked pretty bad."

"I'm glad that they weren't your drugs, Matt," she said. "But even if they were, I hope you feel like you could talk to me about it."

Matt nodded as his Mom stretched out her arms and gave him a hug. He already knew that he could talk to her about anything. But it felt good to hear the words just the same.

"I guess you can have your Sundays back now," she said. "I don't expect you to go to Mr. Evans' sessions anymore."

"I guess so," he replied.

chapter seventeen

Every student at South Side seemed excited about the fact there were only two weeks of school left before the start of summer vacation. But the Stingers still had some unfinished business on the baseball diamond. On Thursday afternoon, the entire team, dressed in full uniform with their cleats slung around their shoulders, marched the twelve blocks to nearby Central Middle School for a must-win match-up against the Wildcats.

It was a must win because one loss and South Side was mathematically out of contention for the playoffs. The team was 5-1 and technically tied with both Middleton and Churchill. But because of the league's complicated tie-breaking formula, the Stingers couldn't win the title if they finished in a tie with either team. Matt had fervently done all the calculations at home on Wednesday night. South Side's only hope was to win both its final games and cross their fingers that the Marauders and Bulldogs lost at least one each. In that case, the Stingers were in.

When the team arrived at Central, Coach Stephens told his players to take a seat in the dugout. The Wildcats were already running through infield practice. "Listen up, people," Coach said. "I'd hoped that we would be able to control our own destiny but we can't. In order to make the playoffs, we have to get some help along the way. All we can do now is play our best baseball of the year during our last two games and hope things break our way."

The Stingers were particularly focused today as Coach cracked out ground balls to the infielders and towering flies to the outfielders. The infielders' throws to Dave Tanner at first were crisp and smacked loudly into his glove. The South Side team seemed ready to do its part in this playoff push, Matt thought to himself.

The umpire called time, and both teams returned to their dugouts. Coach Stephens, as usual, had waited until just prior to game time before hanging the lineup sheet up on the dugout fence. Out of habit, Matt motioned to Charlie to hand him the clipboard. Better make sure the lineup is correct on the score sheet, he was thinking.

"You might want to check Coach's list," Charlie said, nodding toward the dugout fence.

Matt wheeled and looked. There was his name, penciled in at second. He was starting a middle school baseball game for the first time. Coach had moved Kevin Archibald to shortstop to take the place of Jake, whose parents wouldn't let him play anymore this year. Matt felt sorry for Jake but he was pumped to be playing instead of keeping stats.

The game that followed turned out to be the best of the season, for both Matt and the Stingers. In his debut as a starting second baseman, he went three-for-four, including a triple into left field. He didn't make any major mistakes at second, and South Side rolled to an easy 12-3 decision over a decidedly inferior Wildcats team.

Even more impressive, the victory had come without Jake and his powerful bat in the lineup. The Piancatos did consent to let their son tag along with the team to Central, though, and as the Stingers walked back to South Side, Jake seemed as happy about the victory as any of the guys who had actually played.

"Matt, you were stroking it out there today," Jake said enthusiastically. "Your hitting is miles better than it was at the start of the season."

Jake and Matt were walking near the end of the line of players, just ahead of Charlie, who because of his brace brought up the rear of the contingent.

"I had some help," Matt said. "From my personal

hitting coach." Matt flashed a look back at Charlie. He was straining under the weight of a large equipment bag, but he was grinning at the same time.

After supper that night, Matt tuned his bedroom clock radio into KSWT, the local news radio station. He knew they would announce the middle school baseball scores at 8:05 PM, providing all the managers had phoned them in.

He couldn't help but feel nervous as the time approached. South Side had done its part and beaten Central. But to stay alive in the playoff race, it would need both Middleton and Churchill to drop one game before the end of the year.

Matt listened to the entire sportscast, which listed off major league scores and golf results, before the announcer said, "And turning to middle school baseball league action, the South Side Stingers had no problem pounding the Central Wildcats 12-3. In other games..."

Matt felt his stomach flipping about.

"...the Manning Minutemen upset the league-favorite Churchill Bulldogs 4-3..." Matt's heart soared. Manning beat Churchill! Unbelievable! "And the Middleton Marauders easily downed the North Vale Nuggets 6-2."

Just as quickly as his spirits had risen, they were dashed by the news of the Middleton win. Matt clicked off the radio. Well, at least Churchill had lost. There was still a chance for the Stingers on Monday. All they had to do was defeat the visiting Mandela Lions in their final game and then hope that Central, by some miracle, could beat Middleton.

Coach Stephens gathered the team together on the pitcher's mound before Friday's practice. "We're just going to have a short one today, boys," he said. "There's not much we can drill on now. I know you'll play well Monday against Mandela, and the rest is out of our hands. So let's have a good, crisp practice today and then get some rest on the weekend and be ready to come out hard Monday."

There was plenty of optimism in the Stingers as the ball zipped from player to player during the work-out, which everybody was keenly aware could be the last of the season. Matt approached Charlie in the locker room afterward. "Got any plans tomorrow?" he asked.

"Why?" Charlie asked.

"I feel like I could use a little BP," Matt replied, using the major league abbreviation for batting practice.

"I'll be there," Charlie said. "For my usual fee, of course."

Matt laughed. Charlie, of course, would get no pay for helping him. But the two had developed a strong relationship and a common sense of humor during their Saturday morning practice sessions. Matt had also developed a ton of respect for Charlie, who seemed to get more done on one-and-a-half legs than most kids did on two.

That night Matt had a brainstorm. After supper he took five dollars out of his dresser drawer, climbed on his bike and rode the eight blocks to Wong's Grocery. Once there, Matt parked his bike's front tire in the metal rack before swinging open the white screen door with the 7-Up logo on the wide handle. He walked inside the cluttered store with the soft, hazy lighting and the dual aisles of penny candy. Phil wasn't there, but his grandmother was.

Seeing Matt come in, she hustled out from behind the counter and down an aisle toward him. As usual she was dressed in a baggy white sweatshirt and running shoes. Her eyes lit up as she addressed Matt. "Hello, Lucky Boy," she beamed.

Matt had been "Lucky Boy" to Phil's grandmother almost since she had first laid eyes on him. He wasn't sure exactly what the nickname meant but he knew she used it because she liked him.

"I just came to buy something for a friend," Matt said, already knowing precisely which shelf to look on. He and Phil were extremely familiar with the location and selection of all the treats in this store. He picked out the chocolate and coconut cookies that Phil and he had gorged themselves on during many a night of video games. "I'll take these for my friend," he said.

"Must be good friend," Phil's grandmother replied with a twinkle in her eyes as she made change. They both laughed.

The next morning, Matt grabbed the cookies, his bat, helmet and batting glove and rode his bike to South Side. Charlie was there, all set up and ready to go, as usual. After hitting 100 balls, Matt signaled to Charlie that he had had enough. The two rolled the pitching machine back into the locker room together. "Before I go, I've got something for you," Matt said.

"For me?" Charlie asked.

"Yup," Matt replied, fishing into his equipment bag for the box of cookies. "I figured if Andrea can make you cookies, the least I could do is *buy* you some."

Charlie was clearly pleased. It wasn't so much the cookies as it was the thank-you they implied.

"Thanks," he said, "for not using me as a guinea pig for your own baking, that is."

"Well, you've helped me out a lot this year," Matt said. "How did you get to know so much about hitting, anyway? Besides reading books, I mean."

Charlie explained that his uncle Pete had played in Kansas City's minor league farm system for a few years. "He showed me a lot of stuff," Charlie said. "I want to be a coach some day myself."

"Oh, I get it," Matt laughed. "So I'm your guinea pig when it comes to batting practice."

Matt rode home slowly, feeling good about doing something nice for Charlie and about how his hitting had come along since the start of the season. It also felt great that the whole mess with Mom and Officer Peters and Joker had been straightened out. The only downer about the whole thing was Jake. He couldn't play for the rest of the season. That was bad enough, but now Jake had to attend that drug and alcohol counseling too. Worse yet, it was Mr. Evans—Marcia's dad—running the sessions. Matt knew Jake felt kind of weird and embarrassed about going there and facing Mr. Evans tomorrow. That was when he came up with his second straight great idea of the weekend.

chapter eighteen

"You're up and about awfully early for a Sunday," Mom said. She was just getting up herself, but Matt had already finished breakfast and was putting on his shoes.

It was 9:30, and usually Matt and his Mom liked to sleep in on Sunday mornings. But Matt had a plan today and he had to get going. "I'm going out to meet some friends," he said to his Mom, kissing her on the forehead as she scanned the *Post*. "I'll be back in a couple of hours."

Matt grabbed his bike from the garage, strapped on his helmet and pedaled the six blocks to school. He wanted to get there early, at least a few minutes before 10:00 AM.

At 9:55, he spied Jake, heading into the front doors of the school, a look of controlled dread on his face.

"Jake!" he called.

"What are you doing here?" Jake asked. "I thought you'd be off the hook for this."

"I am. But you're here, right? I thought I'd keep you company. Besides, Evans isn't that bad after you get used to his lame jokes."

Matt watched as most of the tension drained out of Jake's face and a little of the usual happy-go-lucky glow returned. "Thanks, man," he said. "I was feeling kind of weird about being here with Marcia's dad."

They walked together into the classroom, where most of the kids in the session and Mr. Evans were already gathered.

"You must be Jake," Mr. Evans said, holding out his hand. "Marcia's told me about you."

Jake gulped. Matt wondered where this was going, but Mr. Evans quickly put everybody at ease.

"Don't worry, Jake. As I told your friend Matt here, everything that goes on inside this room stays inside here. And we're starting with a fresh slate. I'm just here to give you some tools to deal with some of the things you might run into."

Jake nodded. He and Matt grabbed the last two seats in the first row.

"We've got a couple of special guests here with us today," Mr. Evans said, addressing the entire group and pointing to the door of the classroom.

Matt heard a sharp bark as Officer Neil Peters and Joker stepped through the door.

"These two police partners are responsible for plenty of anti-drug work in our city," Mr. Evans said.

"So I thought it would be helpful and informative if Officer Peters and Joker came to speak to you this morning and give you all a police perspective on drugs. Of course, Officer Peters will be doing most of the talking."

The kids groaned at Mr. Evans' typical teacher's weak humor. But they were impressed with the sleek black German Shepherd heeled tightly at Officer Peters' side. When the policeman stopped at the front of the class, the dog stopped as well, sitting proudly in front of the group.

"Joker and I have been partners for about eight years," Officer Peters told the group. "You may have seen him work from time to time in and around your school. He's a drug-sniffing dog, specially trained to be able to detect the scent of things such as marijuana, cocaine and heroin even if they are well-sealed and inside containers."

Officer Peters went on to explain how Joker had been trained and how he wasn't like an ordinary pet. "I would trust Joker with my life," he told the group. "And he has to trust me with his."

After he had spoken for a few minutes about the way he and Joker work together, Officer Peters put Joker in a "down" position and addressed the group with a serious look on his face.

"I know some of you have already tried drugs, which may be why you're here," he said. "And some of you have been offered drugs, like marijuana, and haven't known quite how to handle it, right?"

A few heads nodded around the room.

"Well, I'm going to give you a few pieces of advice," the officer continued. "You do what you want with them, but remember, I've seen a lot of kids mess their lives up pretty good by getting mixed up with drugs and the wrong crowd."

Officer Peters cleared his throat. "The first thing I'd say is be brave enough to turn it down," he said. "I know kids might call you names or stop hanging out with you unless you smoke some weed with them or whatever. But you know what? It's your decision. Nobody else's. If you decide you don't want to do something, then they'll respect that if they're good friends. If not, maybe they're not as good friends as you thought."

Matt's mind wandered back to the night at Long Lake. He was pretty sure Jake was thinking the same thing too.

"The second thing is this," Officer Peters continued. "If you do try something like marijuana, that doesn't mean you're a bad person. Kids experiment. Sometimes they make bad choices. Just don't compound that by making more and more bad choices."

"The last thing," he added. "Is trust the people you've always trusted. Trust in your parents, your teachers, your principals, your policemen. We're all here to help, even Joker."

Matt and Jake stood in the parking lot where Jake's dad was going to pick him up. "Thanks for coming," Jake said.

"No problem, man. I've always got your back."

Matt couldn't resist asking Jake the question he had been wondering ever since that night on Long Lake. "What's it like, anyway?" he said.

"What's what like?" Jake replied.

"You know, smoking a joint."

"It's different," Jake said. "The first time, I didn't feel anything special, just lousy in my lungs from inhaling the smoke. But the next couple of times...I don't know how to describe it. It definitely relaxes you. It makes everything seem funny, and you sort of get spaced out and find weird things interesting.

"But I'm not going to do it again," Jake added. "My parents said there would be no sports for me if they caught me. It's not a tough choice between those things."

"I was scared to try it," Matt admitted. "I thought maybe you figured I was being a wuss that night on the beach."

"Naw," Jake said. "At least you had enough guts not to do it."

The Piancatos' red station wagon was now pulling up to the school. Jake stuck out his right hand and shook Matt's. "Thanks again, bud," he said.

chapter nineteen

The South Side Stingers had just one game left on their schedule. But if they were both good and lucky, their season would extend beyond this Monday afternoon home date with the Mandela Lions.

It was South Side's final game of the regular season. The team had a six to one record, tied with the Middleton Marauders for first place in the city standings. Only one problem—Middleton had the edge in the tiebreaker between the two teams since it had beaten the Stingers 3-2 on that home run by Gus Martinez.

That meant South Side had to win this afternoon and then hope that the Central Wildcats could somehow upset the Marauders in a night game a couple of hours later at Central Middle School.

Mandela, named after the great South African leader Nelson Mandela, was the newest middle school in the city and didn't have an established baseball program. But the suburban school drew students from a huge area and consequently had a lineup full of talented, if inexperienced, athletes. This game wouldn't be a pushover.

After taking infield practice, Matt was standing, watching Mandela take its turn when he heard a voice shouting from the stands. "Hey, Matt, over here."

It was Andrea. She was dressed in a white tank top and cut-off jeans and despite the fact it was early summer her skin had already tanned a light brown. Combined with her blond hair and blue eyes, Matt thought it made her even cuter.

He walked over to the South Side dugout, where she was leaning over the fence. "I heard that Jake cleared everything up," she said. "I'm glad. I also heard that you went along on Sunday, anyway."

Matt nodded. "You've got pretty good sources," he joked.

"That was nice of you, Matt. I bet Jake appreciated it."

Matt felt himself blushing once again. Four rows up in the stands, he noticed his Mom sitting with the Wongs. He hoped she didn't see him with Andrea; otherwise, there would be a lot of questions later. "Well, I better get to the dugout," he said. "I'll talk to you after, okay?"

Coach Stephens posted the lineup on the dugout fence. For the second straight game, Matt was starting at second base. Inside, he was particularly excited because both his Mom and Andrea were here to see it.

Despite Mandela's lack of experience, the game was extremely close. Steve White was once again pitching for the Stingers while Jamaal Baker, a long, lean, seventh-grade fireballer was throwing for Mandela. By the sixth inning it was still scoreless, a combination of both pitchers throwing extremely well and the infields playing sharply.

Matt hadn't fared well at the plate at all. Although his hitting had improved, he was nervous this afternoon. Baker was one of the fastest pitchers he had seen all season and he was just wild enough to scare most of the South Side hitters out of standing in the box and taking solid cuts.

In the top of the sixth, Baker himself was at the plate, facing White. And watching from the dugout it seemed to Matt that White was taking this matchup personally, much as he had done with Jake in that practice session before the season. He seemed to be throwing his entire body off the mound, trying to get some extra speed. Matt sensed that White was losing control of his emotions, but Coach Stephens didn't seem ready to pull him. Besides, without Jake in the lineup, the Stingers didn't have a sure-fire closer ready to step in.

Facing his pitching rival at the plate, White got behind 3-0 in the count. Now he was in trouble. He had to be good with this pitch, and Jamaal Baker knew it. The Mandela hurler was waiting for White to groove one and, when he did, Baker parked it over the right-field fence with a powerful swing. It was 1-0 Mandela, and the stands at South Side fell almost dead silent.

That was all the runs the Lions could manage in their half of the sixth, bringing South Side up to the plate. But Baker was still a force on the mound for Mandela, striking out Phil, Howard Berger and Dave Tanner in order.

It was now the top of the seventh in South Side's final game of the season and Coach Stephens knew the Stingers couldn't afford to put Steve White back on the mound. He had pitched well, but he was out of gas. The coach rubbed his chin and then made his decision. "Berger," he barked. "You're throwing this inning. White, go to third."

Howard Berger, a slope-shouldered redhead with a serious face, gulped. This was a pressure situation to be thrown into. Normally, South Side would have ridden Steve White all the way to the end of such a close game. Either that, or Coach Stephens would have moved Jake in to pitch the last inning. But Jake wasn't available. So Howard Berger was the man on the spot.

Berger walked slowly to the mound. Matt watched as Phil joined him there, his catcher's mask tilted up on his forehead so he could speak with Howard. The two talked for about thirty seconds, then Phil patted Howard on the back and ran behind the plate. After a few warm-ups, Berger was ready to go.

The Mandela dugout was pumped up. The Lions weren't in the running for a playoff spot, but they were clearly enjoying the chance to play spoiler on the Stingers' own field. Matt could tell the Mandela players and their coach sensed they would be able to jump all over Howard.

The Lion hitters were swinging away from the start. The first batter lined sharply toward third base. But Steve White had gotten a jump on the ball and his diving snag on the hard shot was the first out for South Side. Now just two more to go.

The first out and the chatter in the South Side infield made Howard suddenly seem more confident on the mound. He reared back and threw a hard first pitch to the second Mandela batter, who promptly launched a sharp single to shallow center field.

Now the Lions had a runner on first and only one out. They were already up by a single run and were looking to add some insurance. Matt glanced over at the Stingers' dugout and noticed Coach Stephens. He looked concerned.

Berger's sudden confidence seemed to have dissipated with that single pitch. Now he was wiping his brow and shaking his head. Phil looked at the plate umpire. "Time!" the ump called out.

Phil strolled up to the mound, baseball in hand. He chatted with Berger for a few seconds, then patted the pitcher on the back and handed him the ball. Phil was doing his job as the catcher and leader on the field. Berger once again had a smile on his face.

The reliever wound up and delivered a high fastball, slightly inside. But the Lions' batter swung hard anyway and the result was a hard-chopped grounder straight at Matt. He got a bead on the ball, charged it and gloved it smoothly. Mindful of the lead runner, Matt pivoted and tossed the baseball to Kevin Archibald who was covering the bag. Archibald jumped high to avoid the slide of the Lion runner and, in mid-flight, gunned the ball to Dave Tanner at first for the picture-perfect double play.

The play drew a huge cheer from the South Side stands. Matt looked up into the bleachers and saw his mom, smiling and waving at him. He scanned a few rows down and spotted Andrea clapping wildly.

The Stingers ran toward the dugout, eager to put their last at-bat to good use. Archibald was up first and he patiently drew a walk from Jamaal Baker who hadn't lost a bit of his speed but was growing increasingly wilder.

South Side had a runner aboard with Steven White coming to the plate. Jamaal smiled when he saw his pitching rival was next to face him. White grinned back. Matt knew that Steve would be pressing hard on this at-bat.

He was right. White was trying too hard to be the hero. In just five pitches he was on his way back to the dugout, having swung for at least two deliveries that would have clearly been balls. Pete Winters, the Stingers' left fielder, was next. He worked the count to three to two but then watched as the umpire inexplicably called a pitch that was well outside for a third strike.

The groans from the South Side dugout were audible. But Coach Stephens was having none of that. "Quiet, guys," he growled. "The ump made the call. Now let's play baseball."

Matt was already out of the dugout and in the warm-up circle, swinging away. He was up next with South Side's entire season riding on this at-bat. He had been mentally timing Jamaal's pitches while he waited for his turn. This kid was faster than anybody he had faced all season.

The walk to the plate seemed like it took about twice as long as usual. And suddenly, the noise in the bleachers, the buzz that had been there all game, was gone. It was so quiet, Matt could swear he heard spectators breathing.

He stepped into the box, got set and raised his bat up behind his shoulders. Baker wound up and uncoiled his long sinewy body. The ball arrived so fast that Matt barely had time to move away from a chin-high fastball that had come within inches of hitting him.

Ball one. It hadn't been a strike but it had Matt second-guessing, which was what Baker had intended. The next pitch came hard again, but this time it was right down the middle. Matt couldn't help himself. He had jumped backward, away from the plate, before he had even realized what he was doing. "Steeeerike!" the umpire yelled.

Matt stepped out of the box and shook his head. He was angry with himself. He took the sign from Coach Stephens at first base, telling him to hit away if the pitch was good. He looked in the dugout and found the face of Charlie, pressed against the wire mesh. "Like you can, Matt," Charlie yelled. "Like you can."

Matt mulled the words over in his head. If anybody knew what he was capable of, it was Charlie, having worked with him on all those Saturday mornings this year.

He stepped back into the batter's box, determined not to flinch at the next pitch. This one was well outside. The count was two and one.

Baker wound up again and delivered. The pitch was high and inside, and scarily fast. But Matt knew it wasn't over the plate. He resisted the urge to swing and took the pitch. "Ball three!" the ump screamed.

"Make him pitch to you, Matty," yelled Coach Stephens. "Make him pitch to you."

At the same time he was yelling for Matt to have an eye, Coach Stephens was signaling him to swing away. He knew that Baker would have to offer up something good on this next pitch. The Mandela pitcher couldn't afford to walk Matt and have two runners on base.

He was right. Baker wound up and delivered a blistering fastball headed right up the middle. Matt didn't have time to think or even blink. He simply reacted, swinging as hard as he could through the heart of the plate.

Crack! The ball rocketed off his bat, heading high over the first baseman's head and deep into right field. Matt was off and running hard and so he didn't see the ball bounce sharply off the white fence. Coach Stephens was sending him on to second so he kept running, oblivious to the fact that Archibald was coming home from third.

The Mandela right fielder fired a hard throw to-ward the plate, but it was too late to catch Archibald, who crossed home standing up. Meanwhile, Matt had been waved on to third. The Mandela catcher whirled and threw, trying to pick him off. It might have worked if the throw had been on target, but the ball sailed over the head of the third baseman. Winters motioned with his arms for Matt to take home.

The left fielder had been backing up the play, so the ball didn't make it far. He planted and threw toward the plate as Matt streaked in. About ten feet from home, Matt instinctively went into a slide, steaming over the plate just before the catcher's mitt tagged his hip.

"Safe!" the umpire bellowed, his arms spread outward. South Side had won the game, and Matt had provided the winning hit.

The Stingers dugout emptied, all of the maroon and white players circling Matt and slapping him on the back. Charlie limped out behind them and watched with a satisfied look on his face.

Matt was being jostled and pushed and noogeyed by his teammates, but he managed to shake free and yell at Charlie. "Saturday morning special, Charlie," he said.

Charlie just smiled.

chapter twenty

Nearly lost in the wild celebration of the South Side win was the fact that the Stingers still hadn't clinched a playoff berth. They still needed Central to beat Middleton in tonight's final game of the season if they wanted to finish first and make it into the regional tournament.

Because the Central Middle School diamond had lights, the league had scheduled this game between the Marauders and Wildcats for a 7 PM start. So the entire Stingers team had time to shower and change and walk the dozen blocks together to Central to watch the game that would decide their fate.

Coach Stephens couldn't join them. "I put enough time in with our South Side games and practices," he said. "I think I'll go home and spend some time with my family. I'm sure you'll all let me know tomorrow how it turns out.

"But let's remember one thing," the coach continued. "No matter what happens at Central, you guys had a great season. Going 9-1 in this league is tough. You accomplished a lot, whether we're in the playoffs or not."

Although everybody was happy with the victory, the Stingers were a quiet bunch as they made their way to Central. Matt could sense that everybody was nervous. It wasn't easy to watch somebody else decide how your season was going to end.

They sat together in the bleachers, waiting for the game to begin. David Martinez, the junk-ball specialist, was on the mound for Middleton. Central was throwing a tall, skinny seventh-grader named Willis Brown. Matt groaned inside when he saw Martinez was pitching. Central would be hard pressed to win this one, he thought.

The game was about to start when Matt noticed a group of players coming up the steps of the bleachers toward them. It was the South Side girls' softball team, who were heading to the regional tournament the following week in Eton.

They were in full uniform, and Andrea was leading the way. "We came to root for you guys," she said, sitting right beside Matt in the bleachers.

"But we're not even playing," he said.

"So, we'll cheer for Central."

The girls proceeded to cheer and whistle and clap for every good play the home-field Wildcats made. Normally, Central didn't draw many fans. This was probably the loudest support they had enjoyed all year.

The cheering seemed to pump up Willis Brown, the slender seventh-grade pitcher on the mound for Central. Through six innings, he was nearly flawless, throwing surprising heat and racking up eight strike-outs. And when the Middleton hitters did touch him, Central's fielders managed to get their gloves on the ball and make snappy plays to back him up.

Meanwhile, David Martinez was at his junk-ball best on the mound for the Marauders. The Central batters were twisting themselves into knots trying to figure out his baffling combination of off-speed pitches and curves.

The teams were scoreless heading into the seventh inning. And as each inning had passed without the Marauders scoring, the Stingers in the bleachers had grown more excited. Maybe Central did have a chance for the upset after all. Maybe, just maybe, South Side would be going to the post-season.

In the top of the seventh, though, bad luck struck Willis Brown. The freshman Central pitcher who had been so solid through six innings, beaned David Martinez, his pitching rival and the first batter of the inning, with a fastball in the shoulder, giving Martinez a free ticket to first base.

On the very next pitch, he grooved a fastball up the middle to Gustavo Martinez, David's much larger older brother. That proved to be a bad idea. Gus swung hard and drove the baseball deep into left field. Central hadn't been respecting the elder Martinez as a heavy hitter. The ball sailed over the Wildcat fielder's head, bringing David Martinez home. Middleton led 1-0.

The Stingers' visiting cheering section in the stands groaned. Steve White stood up and booed loudly, drawing some dirty looks from the Middleton parents. Matt was embarrassed, but he didn't know what to do about it. This was horrible sportsmanship on Steve's part.

"Sit down, White!" barked Jake who had walked over with his teammates for the game. "No need for that kind of stuff, right?"

Matt was proud of Jake. He was just a seventh-grader but he had developed into a leader on this South Side team, even if he hadn't been able to play the final two games of the year.

Middleton was unable to score again that inning and so, heading into the bottom of the seventh, the Central Wildcats trailed 1-0. If the Marauders could hold on, they would finish the season in first place and head to the regionals. If they couldn't, South Side would get that honor instead. Matt was so nervous sitting in the bleachers he could hardly breathe.

Matt felt a hand grab his as David Martinez finished his warm up pitches for Middleton. Sitting beside him, Andrea had locked the index and middle finger of her left hand through the last two fingers of his right. He stole a glance into her blue eyes. For a second, even though the game in front of him would determine his team's playoff fate, Matt wasn't thinking about baseball at all.

That changed as Martinez began throwing to the first Central batter in the bottom of the seventh. Again, he had the Wildcat swinger baffled with his change-up, forcing him into exaggerated contortions and setting him down in four pitches.

But something was wrong with the Middleton pitcher. He clutched his shoulder, where he had been hit by Willis Brown's pitch earlier in the inning. Middleton's veteran coach, Ace Wilkens, headed out to the mound.

The two talked for a few seconds. Martinez shook his head twice. The coach strolled back to the dugout. Now the field seemed to go absolutely quiet just at it had for Matt in the day's earlier game.

Martinez wound up and delivered. The batter swung early but managed to chop the ball down the first-base line. It looked like an easy out, but it went through the Middleton first baseman's legs. The tying run was aboard with one out. There was still life left for the Stingers.

Martinez shook off the disappointment and bore down now on the next batter. In four more tantalizingly wonky pitches, he struck out that Wildcat too. There were two out, with third baseman Stan Hebert coming to the plate for Central.

It was almost too much for Matt and his Stingers to bear in the stands. Watching this drama play out, and not being able to do anything about it, was excruciating. Maybe it would have been easier not to come to the game, to just listen for the results on KSWT.

Martinez dragged things out to supreme dramatic effect. He painted the corners with his change-up and refused to give the Central batter anything decent to hit for the first five pitches. But with the count three and two and the season hanging in the balance for both Middleton and South Side, he had no choice but to throw a strike.

Hebert guessed right. It was the change-up, and he had waited perfectly, turned and absolutely pounded the ball. It rose high into left field, and Matt's heart almost stopped. It was heading out of the park. Central was going to do it—to upset mighty Middleton and send South Side into the playoffs!

But in that flickering second between what he wished for and what would transpire, Matt realized the baseball was soaring too high. Gus Martinez had been running full out toward the fence since the crack of the bat. The towering Middleton fielder stuck out his mitt on the dead run and snagged the baseball just as it was about to clear the fence. The batter was out and Middleton had won. The Marauders were going to the playoffs. The season for the Stingers was over.

Matt looked around at his teammates. Everybody was dejected after being taken for a two-hour emotional roller coaster ride by these two teams. It had been a great game with an unbelievable ending—just not the ending the Stingers needed and wanted so desperately.

Matt watched as David Martinez was mobbed by his teammates. Although he was sad for himself and the rest of the Stingers, he felt good for Martinez, who was as talented a pitcher as he had ever seen.

Then Andrea jumped up from her seat and shouted in full voice: "Three cheers for the Marauders. Hip Hip Hooray! Hip Hip Hooray! Hip Hip Hooray!"

Jake was next. "Three cheers for the Wildcats!" he yelled.

Martinez looked up from where he had been mobbed on the field by his teammates. He waved to the South Side players in a gesture of respect.

Matt looked at Jake, sitting in the stands. He knew his friend had been disappointed by the way his seventh-grade baseball season had ended. But in typical Jake fashion, he wasn't sweating it now. The competition was over, and he was the good sport Matt had known since pre-school.

Then he felt Andrea's hand in his as they stood

together in the stands watching the Middleton celebration unfold. Baseball season might be over, but
summer was about to begin. And Matt had a feeling
it was going to be a good one.

Jeff Rud has worked as a journalist for the Victoria *Times Colonist* for the past twenty-one years. This is Jeff's second installment in the South Side Sports series. He is also the author of *Long Shot: Steve Nash's Journey to the NBA*. Jeff lives in Victoria, British Columbia.